Lindblom

962-9264

CORNBREAD AND PRAYER

CORNBREAD AND PRAYER

DEAN HUGHES

Deseret Book Company
Salt Lake City, Utah

No part of this book may be reproduced in any
form or by any means without permission in writing
from the publisher, Deseret Book Company,
P.O. Box 30178, Salt Lake City, Utah 84130.
Deseret Book is a registered trademark of
Deseret Book Company.

First printing August 1988

Library of Congress Cataloging-in-Publication Data

Hughes, Dean, 1943-
   Cornbread and prayer / Dean Hughes.
      p. cm.
   Summary: The adventures and inner conflicts of a Mormon family in
1840 reflect the events surrounding the founding of the city of
Nauvoo, Illinois, as a place where Mormons could live and worship in
peace.
   ISBN 0-87579-135-2 : $9.95 (est.)
   [1. Mormons—Fiction. 2. Mormon Church—History—Fiction.
3. Nauvoo (Ill.)—Fiction.] I. Title. II. Title: Corn bread and
prayer.
PZ.H87312Co   1988
[Fic]—dc19   88-18853
                                    CIP
                                     AC

For David and Shauna Wright

Chapter 1

Ruth took a long breath and waited in the hallway for a few more seconds. She wanted to appear composed as she walked into the parlor, where her mother and two older brothers were sitting with Mr. and Mrs. Hemstead. She wished that she didn't blush so easily. One more deep breath, and then she opened the door and stepped into the room. She looked at no one, just stood there for a moment.

"Ruth! Look at you!" Joseph said, and all the others were exclaiming in the same way. Ruth was thrilled but at the same time so embarrassed she had no idea what to do.

Finally she looked at her friend, Mr. Hemstead. He had tears in his eyes — although he was blinking and trying not to let her see.

She was suddenly on the verge of retreat, afraid she might start crying herself; but Mrs. Hemstead, with her usual grace, was suddenly next to her. "Come with me," she said. "I want you to see yourself in a full-size mirror." She took Ruth's arm and led her into the Hemsteads' large bedroom, just off the parlor.

"She looks so grown up," Ruth heard Matthew say just as she stepped into the bedroom.

"Stay here as long as you like," Mrs. Hemstead said. "I know what this means to you. I remember my first party dress." She stepped back a little and looked Ruth up and down. "But I was never half so beautiful as you."

"I'm not beautiful, Mrs. Hemstead. I've never been pretty. I'm just—"

"Trust me, my dear. I don't want to make you vain—but you certainly are beautiful." Mrs. Hemstead touched Ruth's shoulder and lingered for a moment, as though she wanted to take Ruth in her arms. But then she stepped back. "Go ahead and look. I'll leave and let you be alone."

Ruth turned to the mirror and saw herself. The dress was too lovely for her; there was no point in her having it. And yet, she had never felt so new and bright. She ran the tips of her fingers down the lovely, smooth satin, royal blue and glistening even in the soft light; and she touched the delicate lace at the neck. She saw the blue of her eyes too, and was struck with her own prettiness—although she knew it was wrong to think so.

She could hear the muffled voices in the other room. "I guess you never think your little sister will be so pretty," Joseph was saying. "She's always been such a scrappy little thing."

"Joseph, what a thing to say!" Mother said. "She's not scrappy. She's just had to defend herself against her big brothers. There's always been a lovely softness about Ruth; I never saw a baby with prettier eyes."

Mr. Hemstead's voice was barely audible. "She's every bit as pretty . . ." Ruth couldn't hear the last, but she knew what he had said. As pretty as Mary. And she knew what Mary had meant to him. She was the Hemsteads' only daughter, who died at twelve, the age Ruth would soon be.

Ruth felt the tears roll onto her cheeks and began working desperately to rub them away, to keep the drops off the pretty satin. She hadn't thought to carry a handkerchief. Would she ever learn?

Ruth longed so much to be a young lady—like the Eastern women she read about—not some scrappy backwoods girl. But she didn't even remember New York where she was born. Her memories were of log cabins in the wilds of Missouri, and worse—mobs of men screaming and cursing and ripping cabins apart, and afterwards, miserable nights out in the open.

Mostly she remembered the dirtiness of it all—arriving in

Quincy, Illinois, in a ragged dress with only one change, and that as ragged as the first. She remembered the weeks that followed, fifteen people huddled in a two-room cabin, sleeping on the puncheon floors with not enough bedding to keep out the cold. She remembered her hair tied up and not washed in weeks, her boots caked with mud, her fingernails grimy. And the constant fear. Would the men come again? Father and her little brother Samuel had died; would someone else have to leave her?

But things had changed. Mr. Hemstead had come to Quincy and offered work to the Williams family. He owned a large farm a few miles north of town, and his sons, all grown and not interested in staying put, had left him. He needed young men to do his work and run his farm, and someone to help Mrs. Hemstead. Matthew had been nineteen then and Joseph seventeen, and both had plenty of farm experience. Mother was still young and strong, able to take over most of the household chores. Ruth could even earn her keep.

The family soon realized, however, that Mr. Hemstead would give much more than he would take. The boys wanted to work, wanted to show they were men; and Mother, more than anything, wanted a safe, warm place to live. Mr. Hemstead gave them all that and paid them besides.

It was all more than they could have expected: a large, stone house with a bedroom for the boys and another for Ruth and her mother. Ruth had never felt so comfortable, so clean. A year had passed now, and for the first time in her life she felt safe.

Out in the parlor everyone was still talking about her. "She's pretty, but she's bright, too," Mrs. Hemstead said. "She'll make quite a place for herself in this world."

Ruth felt chills pass along her neck. She liked to think of herself that way — being someone, doing something exciting with her life. She turned sideways, still looking in the mirror but not admitting to herself that she was hoping for some sign of womanhood in her shape. Why was growing up so slow? She wished she could go to a party, or to a dance—to be seen by someone other than just her family.

"Ruth. Come out now. I think you've looked at yourself quite long enough."

Ruth knew what that meant. "Why does she always think the worst of me?" she whispered to herself. She waited just a bit longer, fluttered her eyelashes to dry the moisture, and then returned to the parlor. She tried her best to show that she was in control. "Mrs. Hemstead, Mr. Hemstead, I can't thank you enough. It's the most beautiful dress I've ever seen."

"Don't thank me," Mrs. Hemstead said, laughing. "Thank Mr. Hemstead. He saw it in St. Louis and said, 'I'm going to buy it for little Ruth. It's perfect for her.' I said, 'Where will she ever wear it?' But he didn't care. He marched right in and told the clerk he wanted it for the prettiest golden-haired little girl in all of Illinois."

Ruth walked to Mr. Hemstead, put her hand on his arm, and then bent and kissed him on the cheek. "Thank you so much," she said. She had never kissed him before. She wasn't sure it was even proper, but he didn't mind; that was quite clear.

In a moment he stood and patted Ruth on the arm. "Don't make such a fuss about it now," he said. He was a tall man with a white mustache and a full head of white hair; his voice was as kindly as his touch. He suddenly walked, rather briskly, from the room.

As he shut the door, Mrs. Hemstead whispered, "He tries to act so correct, but he's soft as a down pillow. That's the first thing I loved about him."

Ruth waited, not sure she should ask. "Tell me about him then. And about you. Was it lovely in Boston?"

"Oh, Ruth," Mother said. "She's told you everything about Boston. You've asked her a hundred times."

"It's all right," Mrs. Hemstead said. "There's nothing I like better to talk about."

"But Ruth thinks too much about parties and fancy socials. She reads those Eastern newspapers until she wears them out."

Joseph was sitting by the fireplace. He smiled at Ruth. "Let her dream, Mother," he said. "She'll marry a man who goes off to preach the gospel two out of every three years and leaves her home with a brood of little children. They'll live on corn-bread and prayer—and sometimes more prayer than cornbread. She better do all her dreaming now and get it out of her system."

Ruth knew Joseph was only teasing. He actually believed the future was bright for the Saints. He thought the Mormon town up the river—the place Joseph Smith had named Nau-voo—was going to be a beautiful city with fine houses. He looked forward to the day when the family could move there.

"Hush, Joseph," Mother said. "That's not respectful talk."

Mrs. Hemstead was laughing. "I think he's right," she said. She looked at Ruth. "When I was your age I dreamed of the parties I would attend—the dresses I would wear. And it all happened. I danced with the finest young men in Boston—in the most beautiful ballrooms—and had my pick of beaus. And then what did I do? I married Mr. Hemstead, who sold a thriving business and moved out to this Mississippi valley country. He painted the picture so pretty I thought I was moving to paradise. And now you see me, an old woman, worn out, not Eve in the garden, but just an old farm wife."

"You're anything but that," Sister Williams said, but then she sighed. "I didn't dance at any such lovely places, but I had a nice home in New York state. Things *were* nicer there. I followed a man . . . " She stopped. "No, that's not true. We made our choice together." She glanced quickly toward Ruth.

Mother always told Ruth not to worry about houses and dresses and fine china. Ruth heard the words, heard them a thousand times, but it didn't change what she felt. She still saw those ballrooms she had read about and all the pretty people.

Matthew had a way of waiting a time and then pronouncing his conclusion on a subject—much the way Father had always done. He was standing by the big fireplace, his back to the fire, his feet set firmly; and he was looking down on everyone else. "I doubt that fancy parties give people so much pleasure as I get when I see the first winter wheat break ground. There are lots of fine things on a farm—things that really mean something."

Mrs. Hemstead sighed. "Oh, Matthew, that's all well and good. But don't underrate what you haven't experienced. They were lovely—those parties. They added some sparkle to life. Out here, every day is too much like the last. Sometimes, now, I shut my eyes and think of the dinners—with such a spread of food as we never see out here in the West—and the grand balls, with a thousand candles ablaze, the men in fine suits, the women in muslin dresses light enough to float away." Her eyes had gone shut.

Ruth was thinking how pretty Mrs. Hemstead must have been then. She was still a striking woman, serene, with quiet eyes; and yet she had a quick smile that made her seem very young at times.

Joseph was watching Ruth again. Her eyes were full of distance, and full of Mrs. Hemstead. He was worried that she was going to have some heartache before she settled for that cornbread and prayer—and that missionary. He could pretty well guess what she was thinking.

And he was right. Ruth was thinking that life didn't have to be all soil and seed; it could be something much lovelier. She touched the satin dress, looked down at the sheen in the glinting firelight. She loved feeling so pretty, so dressed up. She wished she could feel exactly the same way every day of her life.

Chapter 2

Matthew crouched low, picked up a handful of soil—mud really—and squeezed until drops of water fell from his fist. "It's still awful wet," he said.

Joseph was looking at the sky. The sun was going down, and strings of high clouds were stretching eastward, red-orange and rust-colored. "More rain's coming, too," he said.

Matthew looked off in the same direction, watched for a time, and then nodded.

Joseph had been putting off his question, having sensed a change in Matthew lately; but now he decided it was time. "Matthew, we only promised Mr. Hemstead a year, and that will be up before long. Don't you think we ought to warn him that we won't be staying much longer?"

Matthew had a way of listening without seeming to hear at all. He walked a few strides to a place where his boots sucked mud with every step. "These low spots are especially bad," he said. "If we get a break in the weather, we'll have to plow the top of that little rise beyond the creek and at least get something in the ground."

Joseph was irritated. He shouldn't have to come hat-in-hand to Matthew anymore. He was a good two inches taller than Matthew; and yet, Matthew still made him feel like a boy. "It's only fair that we say something to him. He's probably starting to think that we—"

"He talked to me about it yesterday, Joseph."

"Yesterday? When?"

"When he and Mrs. Hemstead first came in from St. Louis. You were feeding the animals, I guess. You weren't in the house."

"What did you say to him? Did you tell him we were moving on to Nauvoo?"

"He did most of the talking, Joseph. He made us an offer."

"Offer?"

"Come up to the house. I want to talk this over. It's not something we can decide in a minute or two."

"I don't understand, Matthew? What kind of an offer? Why didn't you say something last night?"

Matthew blew out his breath. "Because I knew what you were going to say. I wanted to think about it so I would know how I felt before I said anything."

"You mean, before you made the decision and then tried to make me think I was in on it."

Matthew chuckled. "Come on, Joseph. Don't get so excited."

"Just tell me what the offer was. What does he expect of us?"

"Expect? Joseph, the man is willing to give us everything." Matthew turned around, and now he was between Joseph and the fading sun. He folded his arms over his chest and took that firm stance of his, like a giant braced against the orange light. "He wants us to run the farm and stick with him as he gets older. When he and his wife die, the land, the house, the animals—everything—would be ours, just as though we were his sons. We could both do fine here, Joseph. It's what we've dreamed about."

"No. It's what you've dreamed about."

"Well, all right. If you don't want to farm, I could buy you out in time, and that would give you a start on doing something else. Where else could we find a chance like this?"

"But that's not the point, Matthew, and you know it."

"Joseph, think about Mother and Ruth. Do we want to move them back into another drafty little cabin? Do we want to start clearing land and breaking sod when we've got all this?" He motioned to the darkness, his arm swinging through the dim light.

"Matthew, we promised. We told Father we would stay with the Saints."

"I know that. But Nauvoo is only fifty miles from here. All this region will fill up with Saints. Plenty of our people are staying right here. The day will come when Quincy will be a stake of Zion, and you and I can be two of the men who lead the way. I can look over your land while you serve a mission from time to time, and you can do the same for me."

Joseph had to think. Matthew had worked this all out in his own mind, and he made it sound good. But to Joseph it didn't feel right.

"Joseph, we have to think about Ruth. She's blossoming here, doing well in school, growing into quite a young lady. She needs someone like Mr. Hemstead around to give her things we can't. Do you want to take her up to Nauvoo and stick her out on a muddy little patch of land, make her live in a tent while we chop down enough trees to build a place?"

"Matthew, she'll marry a gentile if we stay here. She'll leave the Church for sure. You've watched what's happened to her. All her friends are from school, not a Mormon among them."

Matthew nodded, his face in shadows, that strong neck of his making a solemn gesture. "I know. It's something I worry about, too. I think we can guide her well enough, and Mother keeps her from getting too far off. But if we think that things aren't working out, we'll move on. We won't commit forever — just for another year."

Joseph didn't like it, not at all. He had been looking forward to this planting season, because afterwards he wanted to get on with his life. "Matthew, I want to be in Nauvoo. I think maybe it's my mission to be there. I want to build, and the building is going on right now."

"So is the dying."

Joseph knew what Matthew meant. He knew about the sickness in Nauvoo.

"Joseph, we lost Father, and we lost little Samuel. We've given our share of lives. Mother is still not back to her full health, and it's the ones Ruth's age and younger who seem to have the worst time. The place scares me."

There was nothing more to say. Matthew was not about to change his mind. Ruth would feel the same way, and Mother probably would, too. Joseph felt a loss, some sense of who he was sliding away. "I may have to go by myself," he finally said.

"Well, I can't stop you. Wouldn't try. But I need you here. One man can't do all the work."

"Get yourself another hired man then." Joseph spat the words out, tried to make them hurt.

"Joseph, don't talk when you're angry. You say things you have to take back later."

Joseph did want to be angry, but it wasn't in him. An image came to mind: he saw himself back in Jackson County, pulling Matthew's lifeless body down an endless road. He had been willing to do anything to keep his brother alive. In his own way, Matthew was pulling now, trying to make things right for the whole family.

"Matthew, I want to go have a look at the place," Joseph said. "I need to do at least that. I could leave tomorrow or the next day and be back before the planting starts."

"I don't see the point of that, Joseph."

"I want to see it for myself. And I need to talk to the Prophet. I've made some promises to him, too, and I need to see what he expects of me now."

Matthew stood his ground, then looked out into the darkness as though he could see his land without the light of day. Finally Joseph saw his head bow just a little and heard him say, very softly, "All right. Maybe you do need to do that."

Emmeline Reynolds fell back across the bed and grasped her head. "Oh, Ruth," she said, dragging out the syllables, "it's stunning. It's . . . it's . . . too beautiful for words."

Emmie was dramatic about everything, and so her reaction

was hardly a surprise. All the same, Ruth enjoyed it. What she said, however, was, "Emmie, don't exaggerate. It's not stunning. It's just—"

"Oh, but it is, Ruth." Emmie sat up. "And you are. I never had any idea you could be so beautiful. You're like the ladies in the *New York Herald*."

"Emmie, that's just nonsense." But Ruth stood before the little mirror on Mother's dresser and tried to see as much of herself as she could. "It's just the dress that's so pretty. Anyone would look nice in it."

"No, no. It's perfect for you—just perfect. Your eyes are like . . . like pools of sky."

Both girls laughed. Emmie had borrowed the phrase from a description they had read together in the *Herald*.

"You have prettier eyes than I do," Ruth said, but she was still looking at her own in the mirror.

"Pools of mud—that's what I have."

"Oh, Emmie, they're beautiful."

Emmie dropped back on the bed again, throwing her arms out dramatically. "Tell the truth. Your hair is like spun gold. Mine's brown as dirt. You have skin like cream; mine's hickory bark. I'll never be as pretty as you."

Ruth objected again, of course, but she knew at the same time that she liked looking at herself much too much. Mother was right about that.

"But where can you wear it?"

"I don't know," Ruth said softly. "Maybe Mother will let me wear it to our meetings."

"Your Mormon meetings?"

"Yes."

"Ruth, your Mormon friends would stare at you like someone from a freak show if you walked in dressed like that. Most of them dress in plain old clothes—some of them in rags."

Ruth turned around. "Emmie! That's unkind. You know what our people have been through."

"I'm sorry. But it's still true. You'd be better dressed than anyone there."

Ruth couldn't deny that. Some of the girls—and their mothers—would think she was showing off. But why have a dress like this if she couldn't wear it anywhere?

"Come to church with me," Emmie said.

Ruth had already thought about that, but she really doubted her mother would approve.

"Think of it, Ruth. Justin McKay goes to my church. If he saw you in that dress he'd fall madly in love with you. He'd follow you around like a little dog. If you told him to roll over, he'd roll himself dizzy."

"Oh, Emmie, don't be so silly."

"Really, I mean it. You've got to come."

"Emmie, Justin never pays any attention to me. He's three years older than I am. Besides, I think he likes Victoria Blair."

"Victoria? Are you serious? She has ears the size of cabbage leaves."

"Emmie! She's very nice." Ruth was laughing again. Victoria did have big ears, but such talk was a sin. And yet, the truth was, most of Emmie's charm was that she said things Ruth would never dare to say.

Emmie was still looking serious. "Would you marry Justin if he asked you?"

"Emmie, please. I'm not even twelve years old yet."

"I mean, when you're both grown. Would you marry him then?"

"I don't know."

"He's handsome, and his father has a big farm and a gristmill besides."

"I know that."

"Then wouldn't you marry him?"

"I'd rather marry a man who would take me to Boston."

"Oh, yes, I agree. A rich man. So rich he owned a great mansion. And he would take you to parties with all the finest people, and you'd ride about in a beautiful coach with a coachman up front."

Ruth thought of dressing in beautiful dresses every day, always feeling pretty, always safe. She liked the image.

"Don't marry a Mormon."

Ruth looked up. "What?"

"Don't marry one of those long-faced Mormon men I see around here. They wear such sorry old suits and worn-out boots, and the only thing they want to do is preach."

"Joseph says I'll marry a Mormon farmer who'll go off on missions all the time and leave me with a brood of little children to look after."

"Oh, Ruth, that's what I fear, too. Don't do it. You could marry a prince. You could live in a castle. Don't settle for a log cabin and a little old farm to break your back on. That would be such a sad way to live."

Ruth thought so too. She had seen enough log cabins and little farms in her almost twelve years. And at the same time she was certain it was wrong to think such things and worse to say them.

Emmie reached over and pulled Ruth's collection of newspaper clippings onto her lap. She searched through the box for a minute or so, and then she pulled one out. "Listen to this," she said. "In the center of the theatre were two splendid golden chandeliers with sixty variegated wax candles therein. At the main box entrance were the golden pillars, supporting golden candelabras. These, with the—"

"I know, Emmie," Ruth interrupted. "We've read it a hundred times."

"But think of it. Wouldn't you like to be there wearing that dress? Wouldn't you like to see every head turn as you walked through those golden pillars? Those Mormon men won't take you anywhere. All you'll get from them is preaching, preaching, preaching."

Joseph had said "cornbread and prayer." Whatever the words, the image had no golden pillars, no chandeliers. It was all logs and mud and mansions on high.

Chapter 3

"Joseph Williams, how good to see you." The Prophet wouldn't settle for a handshake. He folded young Joseph in his arms and repeatedly clapped his big right hand firmly on Joseph's back.

Joseph had not found the Prophet at home when he first arrived, and so he had waited out front, sitting on the sunny side of the Prophet's two-story log house. And before long Brother Joseph had come striding up the street—really just a rutted, muddy road—greeting everyone he saw. He looked healthy and strong, so much better than he had in that stinking jail back in Liberty, Missouri. And he was obviously very pleased to see young Joseph.

"Where is your family?" he wanted to know.

"They're on a farm down by Quincy, Brother Joseph. Matthew and I have been running the place for the man who owns it. But I came up here to . . . to look things over."

The Prophet laughed. "Not so sure you want to move here — is that it?"

"It's not that. I—"

"I wager you've heard nothing but bad about this place. People think they'll keel over and die the first time they take a breath of Nauvoo air."

Joseph hesitated. What he wanted was the Prophet's guidance. But he also knew what answer he wanted, so he was almost afraid to ask. "Matthew feels we ought to stay where we are

14

for now. But I'd like to gather here with the main body of the Church. It seems like what we ought to do."

Brother Joseph was not quick to respond, and young Joseph could see that he was giving the matter some thought. "There's no need to hurry up here, Joseph. Where you've worked out something suitable, I would understand if you decide to stay with it for a time."

"But Father told us, before he died, that he wanted us to stay with the Saints. I'm worried that we're getting too settled in where we are."

"You're just working the land for wages, aren't you?"

"For now. But Mr. Hemstead says we can have it all when he's gone. And Matthew wants it. He says we're close enough to the Saints where we are."

"There is that side of it, Joseph. In time, we'll spread throughout all these parts. And a good farm, free and clear, is not an easy thing to come by."

"I know that," Joseph said, "but I want to be here where we can hear you preach, and I want to help build this city. We're too much on our own now. Besides, I don't like what I see in Ruth. She's taking on gentile ways."

"Well, I can't blame you for wanting to be here with the Saints. You'd give up some things if you came here now, but in time I feel sure you'd prosper."

"We've been told that those who lost their land in Missouri will receive a building lot here, free of charge. Is that true?"

"Yes, that's right." But Joseph caught something in the Prophet's voice—some little hesitancy.

"Am I wrong about that?"

"No, no. Not at all." Brother Joseph thrust his hands into his pockets. He was wearing no coat, and his shirt was open at the neck. He looked more like a backwoodsman than a church leader. "We're asking all who can to pay something. We're awfully short on cash here, Joseph. But those who lost everything in Missouri are entitled. Especially in your case. You lost your father. Nobody paid any more dearly than that."

"If we come, we'll pay something."

"That's fine. But plan to pay it as you can. You'll want to get yourself a house built first."

"How much would others pay—those who didn't lose property in Missouri?"

"It's more what people *can* pay. Some pay a hundred, some two hundred. Some have paid much more."

"I'm sure we would want to pay at least a hundred—when we could."

"That's fine. Do you suppose you'll make the move, then?"

Joseph thought of Matthew, and the picture that came to mind was Matthew's big shadow, like a huge oak, roots sunk deep in the soil. "I don't know. Matthew's afraid some of our family will die here. He says we've lost enough already."

"I can't argue with that, Joseph. And it's true, we've lost too many. But we're going to drain out the wet areas, and that will make things better. Nauvoo is not the swamp some people say it is, but we've got lots of springs and wet places. All that moisture makes the air bad. But if we can just get people to leave us alone here, we'll be all right."

"No one will bother us here, will they?"

"I don't know, Joseph. I hope not." Joseph didn't like the brooding look that came into the Prophet's eyes. "Governor Boggs is still stirring things up. It's going to take some good friends here in Illinois to keep me out of another Missouri jail. Our enemies don't seem to give up very easily."

Joseph nodded, and he looked out across the wide Mississippi, flat and gray in the afternoon sun. This seemed such a peaceful place—a place where all the troubles of the past could end. Why were there always enemies?

"But I'll tell you something. We're going to have an excellent city here. We'll build a temple up there on the bluffs, and lots of fine buildings. This area here below won't be anything but nice homes and pretty yards, with gardens and orchards and picket fences. There won't be a better place to live anywhere. If I were in your place, I think I'd move here just as soon as I could work it out. In the long run, you're going to be happier here."

Joseph nodded. "I want to be here. But I'm afraid I might have to split with Matthew and come by myself."

"I wouldn't do that just yet, Joseph. But you might stay on this summer, find yourself work, and start clearing a lot. If you had a good warm house built before winter, Matthew might feel better about bringing your mother and little Ruth here. By summer's end, this will be a much healthier place to live."

"I can't stay now. I have to go back and help Matthew get the crops in."

"Fine. Do that and then come back."

"Is there work to be found?"

"The truth is, work has been a bit scarce. Or at least work that pays." He suddenly smiled. "We've got plenty of the kind that doesn't pay—except in blessings, of course."

"Well, I can use those, but I need some cash, too."

Brother Joseph laughed and slapped Joseph on the shoulder. "I know the feeling, brother. I'll tell you something, though. You might seek out work in one of the wood yards. Your best chance might be with Brother Andrus, near the upper landing by the big stone house. When boats dock, roustabouts are always in demand. And Brother Andrus hauls in logs and chops wood to sell to the riverboat captains. He might need a strong young man like you who has chopped some wood in his day. I doubt he could pay much, but it might be something."

"All right. I'll go see him now. If Matthew knew I had work, he might be more willing to let me come on ahead."

"That's right. I'm sure he would. Go straight up the street. Then, up where you see the markers for Joseph Street, head off left toward the river again. There's not much you can call a street up that way, but you'll see the big stone house there close to the river. Talk to Brother Andrus, and if that doesn't work out, let me know. I'll try to think of something else."

"All right, Brother Joseph. Thank you. I'm glad to be here. I hope I'll be coming back." As Joseph turned, Brother Joseph reached out and grabbed his shoulder.

"Joseph, I'm the one who's overjoyed. It's the young people like you who will carry on the work. You've been in the Church almost from the beginning, and you've grown up strong and willing and loyal. I always knew you would."

"Not everyone was so sure."

Brother Joseph laughed. "Well, not everyone's a prophet. I just wish some people wouldn't prove me wrong. That sort of thing makes me look bad, you know."

"I won't ever prove you wrong, Brother Joseph."

The Prophet's smile gradually faded. "I know that. You'll be with us, no matter what we have to face. I see that in you."

Joseph was embarrassed, but he was thankful he had come. It was worth it to hear himself praised as one of the loyal ones.

"Well, Joseph, I've got business to attend to," the Prophet said. "Why don't you see Brother Andrus, and then come back and have supper with us?"

"Are you sure that's all right?"

"Oh, yes. Emma can stretch a meal as well as anyone I know. I usually bring in a few extras—she almost expects it. We'll have a look at the city plat too, and we'll pick out a lot you and your family could build on."

"I'll come back then," Joseph said, and he was happy at the thought of spending more time with the Prophet and his family.

Joseph found the big stone house, but saw no docks, nothing that looked like a landing. A brother gave him directions to the wood yard, downriver just a couple hundred yards. Brother Andrus was there, and he said he would be happy to take on another man; in fact, he wished Joseph could start sooner. But he paid no daily wages; he paid by the number of cords of wood cut. Joseph said that was fine, that he could chop wood with just about anyone. Brother Andrus smiled at that. "Well, fine," he said. "You take care of what you have to do, and get back as soon as you can. I'll hold a place for you."

Joseph wondered whether he should promise to return, but he told himself he was coming back—whether Matthew liked the idea or not—and so he made the commitment. "Brother

Andrus, do you know the Engberts? I think they live somewhere here in Nauvoo."

"Sure, I know them. They're just under the bluffs, not that far from here—pretty much due east, I'd say. They built a nice little log house. Do you know their daughter—Mary Ann? She's a little spitfire, that girl. And pretty, too."

"Yes, I know her," Joseph said. Joseph was relieved that Brother Andrus didn't mention any sickness—or a marriage—but he was not about to ask.

"Yes, I can see you do know Mary Ann. It shows up in all that color coming into your face. Well, good luck. I hope you're man enough for that one."

Joseph said nothing. He wished now he hadn't asked. He had never admitted, not even to himself, that his interest in Nauvoo included a certain set of dimples and a certain smile he hadn't been able to put out of mind since his days in Missouri.

All the same, Joseph walked due east, approximately up Joseph Street, such as it was. Much of it was overgrown with grass and weeds. Houses were scattered along the way. Some were still being built, and people were housed alongside in tents or lean-tos. Here and there the street slumped into a muddy bog, hard to walk through. By the time Joseph reached the bluffs, his boots were muddy almost to the tops.

He was not sure which house belonged to the Engberts; there were three or four in that location. And then he heard someone call, "Joseph Williams, is that you?"

Mary Ann was looking up over a shabby row of sticks that was meant to be a fence. She had been working in the garden, weeding, and her face was almost as dirty as her hands.

"Oh, hello, Mary Ann. Is this where you live?"

She put her hands on her hips and cocked her head to one side. Joseph could see that she had grown taller and filled out some; she wasn't a skinny little girl anymore. But those lively brown eyes of hers hadn't changed. "Are you saying you walked clear up here just for the joy of it?"

"Well, actually I was looking around to see whether I could see a good lot. We may be moving up here soon. I'm going to have dinner with the Prophet tonight, and I thought I would let him know what piece of land we might like."

"Dinner with the Prophet. You say that like you think you're somebody. Brother Joseph takes in every sorry-looking river rat that comes along. So don't think you're so important." She was smiling, looking mischievous, but Joseph was not sure how to react.

"Well, anyway, I was having a look around. I just arrived today, and I won't be staying long."

"Don't try to act all grown up, Joseph. I know who you are."

"I'm not trying to act . . . anyway. I just—"

"You asked someone where we lived. And you came up here to look for me, didn't you? I knew you would. I've been expecting you for a long time. I knew you wouldn't forget that kiss I gave you back in Far West."

Joseph was stopped cold now. He couldn't think of a word to say.

"Don't look so disappointed. When I wash my face and put on a Sunday dress, I'm one of the prettiest girls in Nauvoo. Everyone says so."

Joseph was not disappointed. He could see beneath the dirt. He could make out the dimples, and the pretty, quick smile. Her hair was messy, but it was still the color of chestnuts, the way he remembered it.

"You look fine to me," he said.

She smiled—nicely. "Well, good," she said. "You're better looking than you used to be yourself. You're almost as handsome as your brother Matthew."

Joseph probably should have taken offense, but he didn't. In fact, his heart had, for some reason, begun to slam itself against its cage like a trapped bird. She actually seemed glad to see him—even if her way of showing it was a little strange. He did wonder, though, if Brother Andrus might not be right. Maybe he wasn't man enough.

Chapter 4

Ruth took care where she stepped along the muddy path, but she kept glancing up at a blue jay that was sitting in the top of a tall post oak not far away. The tree was only just budding out, still more bronze than green, and the bright jay was brilliant blue in the clear air. Ruth thought of herself, in the blue dress.

And then the jay sounded its ugly screech. Ruth laughed. "Only your feathers are pretty," she said.

She followed the path to the road, and then walked the mile-and-a-half trek through the little valley that bottomed into a creek bed. Someone had scattered boulders across the creek, but the water was running high now, and there was simply no crossing without getting wet. Ruth hiked up her skirt and stepped quickly, splashing her way to the other side, and then she stopped to inspect her boots. They were none the worse, maybe better with some mud washed away; but she hated the idea of their wearing out and looking shabby. As with most everything she owned, the boots were a gift from the Hemsteads.

At the crest of the next hill, she left the road and took the path through a grove of trees to the school. The first redbuds were coming out, deep pink in the shadowy woods, and some of the willows were turning gold. A cardinal flashed across the path, a streak of red. Ruth wondered what a dress so blazing red would look like. But that would surely be going too far.

"Good morning."

Ruth was taken by surprise. She looked over her shoulder. It was Justin. He was a little off the path and behind, angling toward her. "Hello," she said, but she didn't stop walking.

"Wait. I'll walk with you."

Ruth had never known such boldness, never even seen one of the boys at school do such a thing. All the same, she stopped. She didn't look back; she merely waited until he came alongside, and then, without so much as glancing at him, began to walk again. She knew she was blushing as bright as the dress she had just imagined.

"Why didn't you walk with Emmie this morning?"

"I don't know. Some mornings we meet. But this morning . . . we didn't." Why could she never talk at such moments? He must think her stupid as a log.

"I'm glad you didn't."

Ruth didn't dare look at him, didn't dare speak. His meaning was all too clear.

"I wanted to walk with you a little."

"Oh, really? Why?"

"I . . . uh . . . just wanted to."

Ruth glanced very quickly. He was as red as she must be. His neck was glowing, and he was swallowing, as though he had hurt something getting the words out.

Neither said a thing after that, not one word all the way to the school. Except that once they broke into the clearing, with the school in sight, Justin said, "Thank you," and hurried on ahead. Ruth was enormously relieved. She couldn't have borne walking up to the school with him, with all too many eyes watching.

But one set of eyes—dark brown—were big as brass doorknobs. And they were hurrying toward Ruth as she approached the school. "Ruth, I saw. I saw the two of you come out of the woods. Was he really walking with you? Did he say something to you?"

Ruth had hardly found her voice. "Not much," she finally said.

"But something. What did he say?"

"I don't want to tell you."

"Oh, Ruth, it's happened. He said he loved you, didn't he? Did he tell you how beautiful you are?"

"Of course not. And don't talk so loud."

"Then tell me what he said. If you won't tell me, I'll know it's a secret, just for the two of you—to hold in your hearts forever."

"Emmie, please." But Ruth was laughing. "It was nothing like that. He just said he wanted to walk with me."

"He said *that*? In those words? Straight out to you?"

"Yes."

"Oh, Ruth. It *has* happened. A boy doesn't ask a girl to walk unless he's in love with her. It's courting—that's what it is."

"It isn't courting. How can it be courting when I'm only eleven?"

"Because he's fourteen, that's why. And he walked with you."

"He didn't *take* me for a walk. He just walked the same way with me, since we were on the same path."

"But Ruth, he doesn't come that way. He had to go out of his way to get to that path. You know that's true."

Ruth did know that, but she wanted Emmie to stop. The whole thing was too embarrassing.

"What else did he say? Tell me every word."

"He just asked me why I wasn't walking with you, and I said we hadn't met this morning."

"Then what?"

"He said . . . well, he said that he had waited in the woods for me to come along."

Emmie's mouth dropped wide open, and she staggered back a step or two. "He said . . . oh, Ruth. He said *that*?"

"Emmie, don't. People are looking at us. Don't say a word about this to anyone."

"He loves you, Ruth."

"Emmie, be still." But Ruth, for the first time, realized that her heart was beating fast. And something inside was saying, "He *does* like me. He does like *me*."

"He's so handsome, Ruth," Emmie said, suddenly sounding wistful. "When he smiles my knees get weak."

"You're the one who likes him."

"I know I do. I love him. I'm desperately, hopelessly in love with him. But he loves you, and he always will. I read a book about a girl like me. It was the saddest book I ever read."

Ruth walked on. She had no patience with Emmie's theatrics at the moment. "Remember. Not a word. Not to anyone."

Suddenly Ruth came to a stop. She heard a shout and then saw some quick movement over by the side of the school, where all the boys were crowding around. Between all the legs she saw two boys rolling on the ground, and then she saw one bring a fist down on the other. At the same instant she recognized the brown coat and the dark head of hair.

"It's him," Emmie said. "He's in a fight. Oh, Ruth, it must be about you. They're fighting about you."

"Hush, Emmie. That's nonsense. I hate fighting." Ruth walked into the school, went quickly to her desk, and sat down. But when she put her hand to her face, she felt the heat, and she hoped no one would notice that she was still blushing.

Ruth didn't concentrate very well that day. Miss Gordon called on her more than usual, apparently to get her attention, but Ruth constantly drifted away. Fortunately, Justin sat at the back of the class, and Ruth didn't have to look at him. Emmie whispered that he had a little scrape on his face, hardly anything; but the other boy, Jackson Cuell, had a lump on his cheekbone, and his nose was all swollen and red. Ruth told Emmie to hush.

Finally, at the end of the day, as the girls walked down the path through the trees—where Justin had appeared that morning—they had a chance to talk privately.

"All right," Emmie said, "now let me tell you exactly what happened. I got this straight from Lester Benzley, and he was there the whole time and saw everything."

"I don't want to talk about it, Emmie."

"That's what you say. But you really do, so I won't worry about that."

Ruth tried her hardest not to smile, but failed. That was all the opening Emmie needed.

"This morning Jackson and Justin walked to school together, but then Justin said he had to go somewhere, and he cut off and left Jackson. Jackson got to school first, so he watched for Justin. That's when he saw you two come out of the woods, the same as I did, and he told all the boys to look. And then up walks Justin and says hello like nothing ever happened. And then Jackson says Justin had been sparkin' Ruth Williams. And Justin says he wasn't either and to shut his mouth. And then Jackson says he didn't have to. And then Justin says that if he didn't take it back, he'd *make* him take it back. And then Jackson says to try it, and that's when the fight started. So they were fighting over you, just like I said."

Ruth was shaking her head. "Hardly. It sounds more like Justin was ashamed to admit he walked with me."

"Well, of course. A boy has to deny something like that. He couldn't just say, 'Oh, yes, I'm in love with her,' to a bunch of boys. He's picked you out, but he can't say so yet."

"He won't pick me out—not even if I stay here until we're both grown."

"How can you say that after what happened this morning?"

"There are some other reasons he would think twice about it, and you know what they are."

"What are you talking about, Ruth?"

"You didn't tell me everything. The fight was about something else."

"I'm sure I don't know what you mean."

Ruth heard what she feared: the tension in Emmie's voice. "Today when we were having lunch," Ruth said, "the boys divided up, some with Justin and some with Jackson. I couldn't hear much of what they said, but I kept hearing the word *Mormon.*"

Emmie kept walking, looking straight ahead.

"That had something to do with the fight, didn't it?"

"Well, yes, but I left that part out because I didn't want you to feel bad."

"Tell me what happened. Tell me the real story."

"I did tell you the real story. Except right after Justin said he was going to make him take it back, Jackson said something about you, and that's why Justin hit him. So he really was defending you, which makes it all the better, and a lot more romantic."

"What did Jackson say?"

"He just said you were a Mormon."

"Emmie, everyone knows I'm a Mormon. He must have said something more than that."

"Well . . . he said you were a crazy Mormon."

Ruth felt a tightness in her stomach. It was what she had feared. Those kinds of insults had been common in Missouri, but Ruth had hoped they were all in the past.

"Is that something lots of people say?"

"I don't know." The tension again.

"Is it, Emmie?"

"Well, yes, Ruth. It is. That's one of the reasons I think you ought to go to my church. I don't know why you want to go to one that everyone thinks is kind of loony. I'm sure Mormons are very good people, and all that, but they do act sort of odd. You'll have to admit that."

"What's so odd about us?"

"Not you. I don't mean you. But lots of Mormons. They just don't act like regular people."

"Emmie, you know my mother and my brothers. They're normal people."

"I know. But you're not like some of the others. Most of them are moving up to that place on the river and trying to make a city just for Mormons. Baptists and Methodists don't do that. Nobody does. We all just live like everyone else. And you do, too; but when you say you're Mormons, people think you're like all the rest."

"Maybe people should just mind their own business."

Emmie let out a dramatic sigh. "Oh, Ruth, I didn't mean to make you feel bad. But I just think you would be happier if you came to my church, wore your beautiful dress, grew up and married Justin—and not some Mormon. My father says that place where all the Mormons are going isn't healthy, and people are dying off like flies up there."

Ruth felt a chill go through her. She had heard about the dying, even though her family had tried to keep it from her. But she hated to think of it. "Emmie, in Missouri, some men beat my father—for no reason. Just because he was a Mormon. He—"

"But no one here would do that."

"Maybe not. But they said we were crazy there, too. They said all the same things you've been saying. And they beat my father. He was sick a long time after; he couldn't get his strength back. Then he got a fever, and he couldn't fight it off. I can hardly remember him; it was when I was just little. But I remember my little brother. The people in Missouri made us leave when it was still winter, and he was sick. He got so weak he died."

"I didn't know that, Ruth. I mean, I knew they had died; I didn't know how. But that's why you should be like other people."

"Emmie, listen to me. It's not fair. There's no reason to take away other people's land and burn their houses and force them out in the cold."

"I know. We won't do that here. Missouri people are just like that. But all the same, why not get along better with people by being . . . well, normal?"

"Emmie, never mind, all right? You'll never understand."

"No, I guess I won't."

They were on the road now, and Emmie would soon be heading up the lane to her house. Ruth tried to think what she could say, some way to explain. But the truth was, Ruth herself didn't understand. Why *did* Mormons have to be so different? Her family seemed to understand; Ruth didn't. Emmie's dream sounded so much better: attending church in her pretty blue dress; sitting there comfortably, never feeling strange or out of place; growing up part of this place; maybe even marrying Justin. Or better yet, escaping to some better place, having a home of her own, knowing she was safe forever.

Chapter 5

Joseph was gone from home four days. He had only spent one night in Nauvoo, but he had made up his mind what he wanted to do. Over and over, as he rode his horse toward Quincy, he rehearsed in his mind what he would say to Matthew and to Mother.

When he walked into the house, his family and the Hemsteads were still sitting around the table, just having finished dinner. Mother had lots of questions about the people he had seen, and about the city, and Joseph answered as best he could; but he held off speaking his mind about Nauvoo until he could have some privacy. The Hemsteads seemed to get the idea in time. They said they thought they would walk outside for a little while.

"Did you talk to the Prophet?" Mother asked.

"Yes. I even had supper in his home. His wife, Emma, sends her greetings." He thought of telling her that Emma was expecting another child before long, but he knew Mother didn't approve of his mentioning — even noticing — such personal matters.

"That's kind of her. I appreciate that. Did the Prophet have any advice for us?"

"Yes, he did." Joseph tried to think of the words he had rehearsed. "He would like to see us gather with the Saints. He said that if he were in our place, he would move on up. He thinks we'd be happier there, and he thinks we'll prosper there in time." Joseph was eating, but he glanced quickly to see Matthew's reaction.

Matthew was careful, however; he looked calmly back at Joseph and said, "Did you tell him we felt we were close to the Saints right here where we are?"

"No. I told him you felt that way. And he said that was one way to look at it. He even said there was no hurry for us to drop everything and rush to Nauvoo."

Matthew nodded, and Joseph saw his satisfaction. He almost regretted the admission. But he knew he had to tell the truth; it was the only fair way.

"I told him Mr. Hemstead had offered us the farm, and he said it was a fine thing to have a farm, free and clear. All the same . . . " Joseph saw Ruth's reaction, her obvious surprise, and he realized this was the first she knew of this. "All the same, he said he would personally rather be with the Saints. He said he thought it would be better for all of us. The wet areas in Nauvoo are being drained, so it will be as healthy as any other place. He has plans for a temple and for a city that will be as beautiful as any in the country. He needs help to get it built."

This had all rolled out rather quickly, not at all the way Joseph had practiced. He suddenly felt he had given all his arguments in a lump, failing to emphasize them with the kind of force he wanted.

"So did he ask us to come, Joseph?" Mother said. "Did he say we ought to come now?"

"No. He stopped short of that. His advice was to gather with the Saints—but he left the decision up to us."

"What about a building lot? Did he say we'd have to pay for land?"

"He said we could have a lot. Because we lost everything in Missouri, we have that right. But he also said he appreciates when people can pay something. The Church is in bad need of money."

"So what did you tell him?" Matthew asked. "You didn't make any promises, did you?"

"I told him we might come, and I picked out a lot. I said

we'd be willing to pay something in time—one hundred dollars, if we can."

"Joseph, you had no right to do that!" Matthew stood up. "I can't believe you told him that."

"I didn't promise anything. I told him I'd come back and talk to you first." Joseph pushed his plate away. His hunger was gone. He had botched this whole conversation, and he knew it.

"As far as I'm concerned, nothing has changed then," Matthew said. "He's left us to think this out for ourselves. What sense would it make for us to give up eighty acres of good farmland and go up there to build a log cabin on a half-acre lot? Where would we get a hundred dollars anyway?"

Joseph hated to have Matthew looking down on him. He stood up and looked him straight on. "Matthew, lots of people are coming out fine on those lots. They're building nice houses. They raise a nice garden, keep some chickens and pigs, and they live all right. Some are buying farms outside of town. It's going to be the finest town you'll ever see. A temple and public buildings, white fences and—"

"That all sounds pretty, Joseph. But it's nothing but a mud hole now. Everyone who's been there says so."

"It's muddy. Sure. But it won't always be that way."

"And what do we have to gain by going up there now?"

"We can help. We can make it what it's supposed to be. We can go hear the Prophet preach every Sunday. Down here we hardly know we're Mormons. We're going to have some serious problems because of it, too." Joseph glanced at Ruth, and everyone knew what he meant.

"How long before the dying starts again? Last summer hardly a family got through without losing someone."

"Brother Joseph says it's not quite as bad as people think, and it's going to get better. He had a suggestion, and I think it's a good one."

"What suggestion?" Mother asked.

Joseph watched Ruth for a moment. He could see her concern now, and her anger. "He said that I should come back after spring planting. He even helped me find work. He told me to come back and earn wages all summer, and put in what time I could clearing our lot. By summer's end I could have the logs ready, and I could get some help raising a house. I'd even have some cash ahead."

"And all we'd have is a breezy little cabin to move into for the winter."

"I've thought all about that, Matthew. I wouldn't build a little cabin. I'd build a nice big house—something like this one, with finished floors and glass windows. After the harvest, you could move up and move right in to a nice warm place. By then the summer fever would be over. We'd be with the Saints, and we'd make the move in a way we could manage."

"Joseph, is that what the Prophet said we ought to do?" Mother asked.

"Yes."

But Matthew was quick to say, "You said it was just a suggestion. He also told you there was nothing wrong with staying here."

"Nothing wrong with it. That's right. But he thinks we would be better off in the long run to move up there."

"Matthew, I think Joseph is probably right about that," Mother said. "I've been feeling concerned lately that we're getting too settled in here. We've always said we would join the Saints once we could. We promised your father that's what we would do. If land is available for us in Nauvoo, then I think the time has come."

"Mother, I just don't see it that way."

"I know. But I do. It's what I feel we have to do."

Matthew's shoulders were set firm and his jaw tight. He stood with his arms crossed for quite some time. And then he said, "Mother, I'll do what you think is best, of course. But I don't think it's something to decide on the spur of the moment."

Ruth felt sick. No one even stopped to think that she might have an opinion. She saw that Joseph was watching her. She was sure he knew what she was thinking, but she didn't care.

"Matthew," Mother said, "this isn't a quick decision on my

part. It's what I've felt we had to do, sooner or later, all along. I think the Prophet has given us the best answer. It's what we're going to do."

Suddenly Ruth was on her feet. "No, Mother. Please. Don't make us go up there."

"Ruth, I'm thinking of you as much as anyone. You'd be better off there, where these gentiles wouldn't put so many false notions in your head."

Ruth seemed to be searching for something to say, some answer. Joseph was struck with the look in her eyes, those pretty blue eyes turned hard, resolved. And yet they were Mother's eyes—Mother's face really. The hair, the tone of her skin, the curve of her jaw, even the tightness in the little muscles by her eyes—it was all Mother.

But Ruth couldn't hold the hardness. Tears brimmed up in her eyes. "Mother, can't you see what will happen to us if we go up there? People don't like us gathering into cities like that. It's the same thing we did in Missouri."

"What do we care whether people like it or not? That's none of their concern."

Ruth wanted to say what she really felt, but Mother wouldn't understand. In her frustration, Ruth suddenly spun and ran from the room and up the stairs to her bedroom. She lay on her bed and sobbed. Why couldn't Joseph and Mother understand? If they gathered into a city, the whole thing would start again—the hatred and the attacks, the burning and killing. It was only asking for trouble.

Downstairs, Mother had watched Ruth run away and then turned to Matthew. "Do you see why we have to go?" she said. "We're going to lose that little girl if we don't find a way to get her closer to her own people."

Joseph had said the same thing, almost in the same words, but Mother sounded harsh. Joseph thought he understood Ruth's feelings. He waited a few minutes, and then he excused himself and followed Ruth to her room.

"Don't baby her," Mother said as Joseph climbed the narrow stairs. Joseph didn't answer.

At the top of the stairs he stopped for a moment near the door of the bedroom. He could hear Ruth crying, and he wondered if he should leave her alone a little longer. But he didn't want to go back downstairs, so he tapped a couple of times at the door, opened it, and looked in. "May I talk to you for a minute?" he said.

"No. I already heard what you have to say."

All the same, Joseph walked in and sat down on the chair near Ruth's bed. She was lying face down, no longer crying audibly, but with both arms pulled under her and her hands under her face. She was wearing a calico dress, the thin fabric now pulled tight against her slim back. She looked delicate to Joseph. "Just let me say one thing, and then I'll leave you alone," he said.

Ruth said nothing, but Joseph hesitated for a moment.

"Ruth, our people are trying to accomplish some things that a lot of people don't care about. That sets us apart. It doesn't make us better, but it *does* make us different in some ways. I know you don't like that, but it's part of what we have to live with."

Ruth suddenly sat up and looked at Joseph. Her face was red, her cheeks creased. "It got little Samuel killed," she said. "That's what it did. And Father, too."

Joseph nodded. She may have looked delicate, but Joseph felt her toughness. "I know. In a way that's true. But there are worse things than death, Ruth. What if—"

"Oh, Joseph, that's just talk. You watched what happened to poor little Samuel."

Joseph somehow hadn't realized that the pain had been that deep, that Ruth was still feeling the loss so much. Or the fear. "Is that what worries you—that more of us will die?"

Ruth's eyes dropped, the lids going shut for a moment. She didn't answer. She was just a little girl, after all. Joseph had not seen that so clearly in a long time.

"Ruth, if we go to Nauvoo we can help build Zion. It's what we have to do. I know it's what I have to do with my life."

"Then do it, Joseph. But why should we all have to go? Mr. Hemstead wants us to stay. It's a good place, and it's safe here."

"No place is safe, Ruth. Not really. There are all kinds of dangers in this world."

"But some places are a lot better than others. And Nauvoo is the worst."

"Ruth, I don't think it's quite as bad as you think, and it's going to get a lot better. I'll tell you something else. If you stay here, you'll end up outside the Church altogether. In a year or two you won't even be a Mormon."

"What's so bad about that?"

"Ruth, how can you—"

"Tell me what's so bad about it, Joseph," Ruth interrupted. She was breathing hard. "No, don't tell me. Just leave me alone."

"Ruth, I know how you feel."

"No you don't, Joseph. Please leave me alone."

Joseph stood up. "All right," he said. "I will for now. But we're going to have to talk."

Ruth said nothing. After a moment Joseph left. Ruth lay back on her bed, but now with her face up. She had never talked to Joseph this way before. Already she was sorry. He had always been the one who seemed to understand her, always the one who cared about her most. Why did it have to be Joseph now who was trying to talk the family into doing such a foolish thing?

"Why do I have to be a Mormon?" she said out loud, and the tears came again.

Chapter 6

The weather was mostly dry the next couple of weeks. Matthew and Joseph were soon plowing and were able to plow every day — except for the Sabbath, of course. On those days the Saints gathered in a rented hall in Quincy, where services were held.

Mother and Matthew had talked things over several times, and they had agreed at least to the beginning of Joseph's plan. Joseph would leave after planting, and he would prepare the way for the family to follow in the fall. Matthew, however, kept saying that they should hold off on a final decision until they saw how everything worked out for Joseph. This attitude irritated Joseph and gave Ruth her only hope.

Joseph went about the planting with little joy. It was tiring work. Every afternoon he watched the sun and longed for it to set. Matthew would work until he could no longer see and then complain that the days were still too short. After he came in the house, he would spend the evening talking about the next day: what sections the boys could plant, how much work they could get done. Joseph knew he still hadn't given up the place.

When school let out for the summer, Ruth didn't see Emmie. One day, however, her mother gave her permission to walk to the Reynoldses' farm and pay a visit. The two girls went to Emmie's room and talked about what they had been doing and about the possibility that Matthew still might win out and keep the family at the Hemsteads'.

"Ruth, have you worn the dress yet?" Emmie asked. "If you move up to that place, I doubt you'll ever wear it there."

"No, I haven't worn it."

"You mean it's just sitting in a box? You'll outgrow it before long and never wear it anywhere, not even once."

"I know." A day never went by without Ruth thinking the same thing. "I suspect that's exactly what my mother is hoping."

"That's not fair. She has no right to do that to you."

"What can I do about it?"

Emmie was sitting on a rocking chair near her bed. Now that some of her older brothers and sisters had married and moved away, Emmie had a room all to herself. Ruth envied her for that. "All right," Emmie said, "I'll tell you what we can do. Next time you come to see me, sneak the dress out and bring it with you." She hesitated, as though she weren't certain about the next step in the plan. "And then, ask if you can come and stay a few nights with me some time. You could go to church with me and wear the dress."

"Mother would never let me do that. She would want me home on the Sabbath so I could go to our own meetings."

"But how could one Sunday make that much difference?"

"It makes a difference to Mother."

"What if I got sick and sent a note that I was down with something and wanted you to come and sit with me?"

"She'd be afraid I'd catch a fever and bring it home."

"All right, then, what about this? What if I fell and hurt myself and couldn't get out of bed? And I needed company for a few days. You could stay on Sunday, and maybe she would think you were doing your Christian duty."

Ruth smiled in spite of herself. It was a wicked plan and she knew it, but she liked thinking about it. "Are you planning to fall down very soon?" she asked.

"As soon as you get the dress over here."

"Who would write the note?"

"I would. But I'll sign my mother's name. I know how she writes. Your mother wouldn't turn her down."

Ruth felt a tingling sensation in her stomach—scared and yet excited—partly at the thought of having a chance to wear the dress, but more because of the deception. "It's a sin to do something like that," she said.

"I don't think so." Emmie pushed a curl behind her ear. "I think it's a worse sin to waste good things. And never wearing that beautiful blue dress would be the biggest waste I can think of."

And so Ruth agreed. The next time she was allowed to go to Emmie's she sneaked the dress out to the barn while Mother was in the kitchen, and then, when it came time to leave, she went to the barn, got the dress, and angled off from the barn to a row of hedge trees that blocked the line of sight from the house. It was all very easy.

As it turned out, the deception worked almost better than the girls could have imagined. A week later, when a young man—Emmie's little brother—showed up at the Hemsteads' with the note, Sister Williams believed it. She came back to the kitchen where Ruth was scrubbing the floor and said, "Honey, I'm afraid your friend Emmie has had a fall and is laid up in bed for a while."

Ruth was so nervous she didn't trust her voice. She nodded.

Mother apparently took this for concern. "It doesn't seem to be anything too awfully bad, but she could use some company. I think a change might be nice for you. I've worked you awfully hard these last few weeks. Finish that floor and then pack up a few things, and I'll have Joseph take you over in the wagon. Joseph likes nothing better than to get away from plowing for an hour."

She could be so strict at times, and yet now she sounded very kind. Ruth felt guilty. She hoped Mother would never find out what a wicked person she was.

On the way to the Reynoldses', Joseph tried to talk to Ruth. But to Ruth, it was more of the same—all the reasons she should be happy to move to Nauvoo. Ruth didn't argue, but she really didn't listen either. When they arrived, Joseph got down and then lifted Ruth down, handed her the carpetbag she had brought along, and got back in the wagon.

Ruth walked slowly and solemnly to the front door of the

farmhouse, but then she heard Emmie's voice from an upstairs window. "Oh, I'm in such terrible pain. Come up, sweet sister, and give me comfort." This was followed by so much giggling that Ruth spun around to make sure Joseph hadn't heard.

Once she was upstairs and could see Emmie's face, Ruth couldn't help laughing herself. "We did it," Emmie kept saying. "We're criminals. We've begun a life of crime."

"My mother never doubted for a second," Ruth said. She was actually uneasy about that, but Emmie was delighted.

"That's because I'm a first-rate forger. Next I'll probably start printing counterfeit bank notes."

Ruth finally gave way. She wasn't going to doubt herself; she was going to have a good time. She really wanted to be more like Emmie, not always so worried about everything. What was so bad about what she was doing, anyway? All she wanted to do was wear her dress. She had a right to do that.

The next few days were great fun. Emmie's parents expected virtually nothing of the two girls. The Reynoldses had lots of hired help, and they rarely asked Emmie to do any work. That meant long days to talk, to pick out tunes on Emmie's pianoforte, and to plan their big day at church.

On Sunday morning the girls got up early and spent hours getting ready. Emmie had a dress—canary yellow—that was almost as fancy as Ruth's. The girls curled their hair and even sneaked some rouge to give their cheeks a little extra color.

"Mother doesn't think girls should paint their faces at all," Ruth said, rubbing the rouge almost out of sight.

"Neither does mine. But we won't think about them today," Emmie said. "If I thought Mother wouldn't notice, I would put on a whole lot more."

"Oh, Emmie!" Ruth said, but she laughed.

"Nature provides," Emmie said, "but sometimes not quite enough. That's when you have to help it along."

"You've been reading too many Boston newspapers."

"I know. I'm a modern woman. Next I'll probably start smoking cigars and chewing tobacco." She turned her head and pretended to spit on the floor.

The image was too much for Ruth—Emmie in her dark curls and her fancy yellow dress, spitting like a man. Ruth laughed so hard she had to sit down, but she was back up quickly, worried that she might wrinkle her pretty dress.

The ride to church was not long, but it was very warm, even under the canopy top on the wagon. The girls sat in the back and kept fussing with their hair and straightening their dresses. "I'm going to look a sight by the time we get there," Emmie kept saying. "I wish my hair had more curl, like yours."

But Ruth had little to say. She was nervous about entering the church as a stranger. Her self-consciousness only grew as she got down from the wagon and walked toward the chapel. When she stepped through the door, Ruth felt eyes on her from all parts of the little building.

Ruth and the Reynoldses found a pew and sat down, and by now Ruth's heart was pounding. She noticed a girl from school, Madaline Rogers, and she nodded to say hello. But Madaline just stared. She was wearing a simple dress, one she had sometimes worn to school.

People were still coming in. The room was warm, and many of the ladies were fanning themselves. Most of the people were farmers, some pretty well off; but no one was dressed so nicely as Ruth and Emmie. Eyes kept turning their way, and more and more. Ruth looked down to avoid the stares.

"You're a sensation," Emmie whispered. "Everyone is looking at you. They think you're the prettiest thing they have ever seen. Did you see how jealous Madaline was?"

"Hush, Emmie. Don't talk so loud."

"Oh, look, there's Justin." Emmie was twisting in her seat. In a moment, Justin and his family walked past the pew where the girls were sitting. They found a place well toward the front. Justin hadn't noticed Ruth as he walked by, but as he entered the pew he glanced back and suddenly stopped and took a second look. He smiled, just briefly, and sat down.

"Did you see that?" Emmie whispered. She giggled. "His eyes almost popped out." Mrs. Reynolds leaned over and told Emmie to be quiet. The minister was ready to begin.

The meeting seemed unusually tedious, partly because of the heat in the room and partly because Ruth could not concentrate on what was said. Reality was upon her now, and she felt terribly out of place.

When the meeting ended, the socializing began. Lots of people stopped the Reynoldses to ask who their beautiful friend was. Ruth had hoped for such attention, longed for it, but now she was only embarrassed. The comments people made only called attention to the fact that no one else was so nicely dressed.

Ruth had almost made it to the wagon when Justin finally approached. "Nice to see you, Ruth," he said. He was not wearing a suit, not even a waistcoat, but was in shirtsleeves. He was holding his hat in his hands, fiddling with it nervously.

"Hello, Justin," Ruth said. She glanced around to see whether anyone was watching. Emmie had suddenly stepped away.

"You look . . . very nice."

"Thank you."

"I'm glad you came," Justin said, but his forehead, which was white compared to the rest of his face, suddenly turned very red. "Do you think you might come again?"

"I doubt it."

"Well, I'll see you at school this fall then—if I come back for another year." He nodded and walked away. Some boys, fellows from school, were waiting not far away, and Ruth knew that he was about to take a teasing.

All the way back to the Reynoldses' place, Emmie chattered about the sensation Ruth had made at church, and she wanted to know every detail of what Justin had said. But Ruth felt distant and strange. She missed her family, even missed her usual Sabbath trip to Quincy. She looked down at the pretty satin as the dust swirled around the wagon, and she suddenly felt a perfect fool for having worn such a dress to a country church meeting.

Ruth changed clothes quickly when she got back to Emmie's room, and she combed out her hair and washed the rouge from her face. She told Emmie she really felt she should go home.

Emmie pleaded with her to stay another day, but Ruth wanted to go. She was about to walk, but Emmie asked her father to give Ruth a ride.

When the wagon pulled up in front of the Hemsteads', everyone was out in front, sitting on the porch in the shade. Ruth hurried, thanked Mr. Reynolds, as did Sister Williams. But no one asked how Emmie was doing, much to Ruth's relief.

Ruth greeted the Hemsteads politely and walked into the house. Mother followed close behind. "Ruth, let me talk to you for a moment," she said. They stepped into the parlor, and Mother asked Ruth to sit down.

"Did you have a nice time?" Mother said.

"Yes."

"How is Emmie doing?"

"She's fine . . . now."

"I suspect she was well enough to go to church then."

This was leading somewhere. Ruth felt trapped. "Yes."

"And you went with her?"

Ruth hesitated a moment. "Yes."

"Did you enjoy the services?"

"They were all right. The preacher didn't talk so long as ours do." Ruth tried to smile.

"Were you beautiful in your blue dress?"

Ruth looked at her mother for a moment, wondering how angry she was. Then she looked down, more ashamed than scared.

"When did you take the dress to Emmie's? You didn't have it when you left the house."

"I took it last week." Ruth's voice was so small it was barely audible.

"Then you planned all this. Was the note a lie?"

"Yes."

"Did Emmie's mother write it?"

"No."

Mother sat for some time. Ruth did not look at her. "Ruth," she finally said, "when I noticed the dress gone, I tried to believe that you wouldn't do such a thing. I'm very disappointed in you. Do you have anything to say for yourself?"

"No."

"Did the dress mean that much, Ruth? Were you willing to lie and deceive just to wear it?"

Ruth was close to tears. She wanted to say she was sorry, to admit that the day had not given her the pleasure she had hoped for. She wanted forgiveness. But she also felt the anger welling up in her. "Mother, it isn't fair. How could I have such a beautiful dress and never once—not even one time—wear it?"

"The answer is, you never should have had such a dress. It was wrong for Mr. Hemstead to buy it for you. You are not an Eastern lady. You are a simple Mormon girl. That dress has made you prideful. You'll never wear it again, I can assure you of that."

On the way home from the Reynoldses' farm, Ruth had reached the same decision. The dress had been wrong, had made her embarrassed, not happy. She knew she would not wear it again. But Mother didn't have to tell her so. "You can take the dress away, Mother. But you won't always be able to decide what clothes I wear—or what I do."

Sister Williams stood up. "Young lady, you will never speak to me in that tone of voice again. Do you hear me?"

Ruth was as shocked as her mother was. She never expected to say such a thing, and now she was desperately sorry. But something in her wouldn't let go, wouldn't let her apologize.

"Ruth, you have lost all sight of what matters in this world. You care more about that dress, and about that silly Emmie, than you do about anything. You'll not see Emmie again this summer. We'll move to Nauvoo this fall, and I just hope that when you get back with the Saints you will begin to set things right in your life."

Ruth had never been so torn and confused. She walked up the stairs to the bedroom and sat down on the bed. She looked toward the window, saw nothing. She still didn't know what she was feeling; she only knew her mother was wrong about one thing. It was not the dress. She knew she wanted something— but it was something more than a satin dress.

"I'm sorry," Ruth finally whispered, but she wasn't even sure what she regretted.

Chapter 7

Joseph was ready to leave. He had planned to walk, but Mr. Hemstead told him to take a horse. He could bring it back in the fall. Joseph thanked Mr. Hemstead and then shook his hand.

"I hope you'll change your mind, Joseph," Mr. Hemstead said, clinging to his hand. "I think you know you've become like family to me. I don't want to give over the farm to strangers. I would like you and Matthew to have it."

"I know, sir. But you know how I feel. I've said it all before."

"Well, yes. I know what you say. I don't pretend to understand it. I never heard of a church that says you have to live in one place or another. That doesn't seem to me to have much to do with religion. But I won't get into all that again. Every man has to decide those things for himself."

"No one could have been better to us," Joseph said. He walked on to the barn, intending to do the last of his packing and then to say good-bye to the family just before he rode off. This leaving he had been looking forward to was not as easy as he had thought it would be.

He was tying down his bedroll and extra clothing when Matthew came into the barn. "You better take this," Matthew said. He was holding out a bank note.

"I have some money," Joseph said.

"I know. But you'll need plenty if you set out to build a house and furnish it."

Somehow Matthew could always make Joseph feel like a

little boy, someone Matthew had to look out for. Joseph reached out and took the note, folded it without looking to see how much it was, and shoved it deep into his inside coat pocket. "Thank you," he said.

"Don't thank me. It's our money for our house."

"You will come, won't you, Matthew?"

"That's the plan right now."

"What does that mean?"

"It means that's what we've settled on. It's what Mother wants, and you want. It's what I've agreed to do."

"But if you had your own way, we'd stay, wouldn't we?"

"Yes."

"And so now you're hoping I'll come back with a bad report, and you can change Mother's mind—or that you can change her mind while I'm gone."

"Joseph, why do you always start up this way? I agreed to move to Nauvoo. I never agreed to like the idea. The biggest worry for me right now is that you'll get sick up there. From what I hear, lots of people are down with the fever again this summer."

"I'll be all right."

"I hope so, Joseph. I really do. I'm scared what might happen to you."

They were standing opposite each other, on either side of the horse. Joseph looked across. He was a little taller than Matthew, but not nearly so strong. He felt that strength; he also felt the concern. It was the quality Father had always managed to communicate. Maybe Matthew was growing into it.

"Thank you, Matthew."

The horse shifted its haunches and then flipped its tail back and forth. The boys were silent for a moment, and then Matthew came around the rear end of the horse, patting its back as he moved. He stood next to Joseph until Joseph, rather awkwardly, turned partly toward him. Matthew put his arm around Joseph's shoulders. Joseph was a little too embarrassed to turn all the way and actually embrace him.

"Joseph, I'll miss you."

Neither boy said any more. Matthew stepped away just a little. He checked the cinch on the saddle, maybe just to do something, but it was the kind of thing Matthew always did. This time it didn't bother Joseph.

Joseph led the horse out of the barn and out to where Mother and Ruth and the Hemsteads were waiting by the house. He shook hands again with Mr. Hemstead and accepted a little hug from Mrs. Hemstead. "Come back to us," she said.

"Well, I'll see you all before very long," Joseph said. He had agreed to return at the end of the summer and report on conditions in Nauvoo and the progress of the house. Then they would settle on exactly the time the move would take place. Joseph would help with the harvest, and help get the farm ready for someone else to take over the following year.

"Joseph," Mother said as she embraced him, "be very careful. Be sure to eat right. Try to sleep up high, on the bluffs somewhere, where the air is good. Someone might be willing to put you up, but don't go into homes where there's sickness."

"You've given me that speech three times a day for two weeks now, Mother." Joseph smiled at her. And then he turned and gave Ruth a hug. "Ruth, I've tried to say some things to you, but I don't think you wanted to hear any of it. You're a little too much like me, I guess."

When he stepped back, he took a long look at her, but he could not tell what she was thinking. She had been difficult to read for some time now. He knew about the forged note; he didn't know what had been said between Ruth and Mother. The only thing he was sure of was that there was still tension between them.

Joseph turned to the horse, slipped his foot into the stirrup, and swung himself up into the saddle. "Well, good-bye, everyone. I'll see you in a couple of months or so."

He urged the horse ahead, but not at a trot. The trip would take a good two days. Joseph was just glad he had a horse.

At the gate he turned to wave, and then he saw Ruth running after him. "Joseph, just a minute."

Joseph stopped the horse and waited.

"Joseph, I'm sorry."

"Sorry for what?"

"Sorry I didn't say anything. I do appreciate the things you've tried to tell me."

" 'Tried' is right. At least you agree that they didn't sink in."

"Maybe some things did." She was looking up at him, squinting against the morning sun. She seemed to have something more she wanted to say.

Joseph waited for a time, and then finally he said, "Well, Ruth, you'll work things out. You're a good girl, and you've been taught what's right. Everyone wondered if I was ever going to get things worked out in my own head, but I guess I finally did." He waited again, hoping she would say something. "I'll see you later this summer, and maybe we can talk again. You do some thinking between now and then, all right?"

"All right."

Joseph nodded, and then reached down and patted Ruth on her pretty hair. He nudged the horse with his knees.

"Joseph."

Joseph stopped the horse again, and he smiled. "Would you say what it is you want to say, little girl. This horse thinks I'm trying to teach it to dance." But now Joseph saw tears in Ruth's eyes.

"Joseph, I'm afraid I won't ever see you again." The tears spilled over onto her cheeks.

"Oh, Ruth, don't say that."

"So many people are dying in Nauvoo."

"Some have, sure. But not so many as all that."

"Why can't you just stay? Why can't we all stay here where we're safe?"

"Ruth, we've talked about that a hundred times already. I do feel safe. The Lord has some things for me to do; I just don't think he's going to let me die right now."

"Then why did he let Samuel die? And Father?"

Joseph smiled. "I can't slip anything past you, can I? Ruth, I asked those same questions until I drove myself half crazy.

And then I just quit asking. The truth is, I don't really believe that the Lord will stop all the bad things from happening in this world. What I do believe is that I have to do what I feel the Lord wants of me—and then if I die, it's all right."

"I don't want to die. And I don't want you to die, either."

Joseph knew the feeling. He remembered his fears back in Missouri, his attempts to take control of what he couldn't even get hold of. "Ruth, don't get your mind too set. Leave a little room for the Lord to work on you. Have you ever tried to pray about all this?"

"No."

"Why not?"

She looked down. "I don't know."

"Will you do it now? Will you pray and ask the Lord what he wants you to do?"

Ruth looked back at Joseph for quite some time, but she looked away when she answered. "I know what I want to do."

"Whether it's right or wrong?"

She didn't answer.

Joseph looked back toward the house. Mother had stayed on the front porch. She was watching Joseph and Ruth. She could not hear their conversation, but she nodded to Joseph, as if to say, "Talk to her, Joseph. Do what you can."

"Will you do two things for me?"

"I don't know."

"Will you ask the Lord to protect me?"

"Yes."

"Well, if you're going to ask him to help me, you can ask him to help you, too—as long as you're already talking to him. Just ask him what he wants you to do. Please. Will you do that for me?"

"Why for you?"

"Well, you say you're worried about me. I'm just as worried about you. Maybe more. Will you do it?"

"All right."

"Good. That makes me feel better. And we'll talk about this some more when I get back."

Ruth nodded and Joseph patted her head again, and then he rode away. "She'll be all right," he told himself. "If she'll just ask, I think she'll get some answers."

But Ruth was thinking, too. She knew what she wanted. She wanted to sit down to dinner with nice people, in a two-story brick house, to feel pretty, to talk and laugh. She wanted not to be afraid. How could the Lord have anything against that? Why was it that Mother and Joseph seemed to think she had to live in Nauvoo to please God, when there were so many other places to live?

Chapter 8

When Joseph arrived in Nauvoo, he went straight to the wood yard. He was nervous that Brother Andrus might have hired someone else by now. But Brother Andrus was happy to see Joseph. "There's work, all right," he said. "In fact, why don't you grab an ax right now and get started. We've got boats coming in every day now, and it's no easy matter to keep up with all we've got to do. I have two men out hauling today, and we'll have another big load of logs coming in before sundown."

"Let me get a place to stay for the night, and I'll be back in the morning."

"Have you only just got here?"

"Yes."

"Well, you can sleep in our shed here, and that'd be good. That'll help keep some of this river riffraff from running off with our wood at night."

"Will people really do that?"

"Listen, son, this may be Zion, but there's an element of folks here that you don't want to tangle with. Some of 'em are here from before. Others come up here because they figure it's a place to hide among the Mormons. But they'll steal anything that ain't tied down, and they don't think much of throwing a man in the river with a rock around his neck, either."

"Sounds like a nice place to sleep, here by the river."

Brother Andrus laughed. "Well, I suspect you can take care of yourself. I'll leave you my rifle, though, and a knife long enough to stab a man from halfway across the river."

Joseph laughed, but he hardly liked the idea. He wasn't sure he would spend many nights in the shed. Mother had said to go to high ground, but he had no idea where he would stay if he went that direction. From what he could see, it was all over-grown with woods.

So Joseph grabbed an ax and went to work. Within a few minutes he was reminded, however, that chopping wood was all too much like plowing a field — hard on the back. And he would be chopping all day for Brother Andrus and all evening on his own lot, if he wanted to get a house built. He also realized that he had been riding a horse for most of two days and was rather worn out.

Late in the day the other two men — Brother Spencer and Brother Frampton — arrived with a load of logs, and all four of them chopped wood until well into the evening. Joseph was so tired and hungry he could hardly stand up. He stayed with it, however, didn't put down his ax until the others did. He wanted to show what he could do. When Brother Andrus finally said he had had enough and was going home for the night, he invited Joseph home for supper. But Joseph said he had some people he wanted to call on.

"Well, that's fine. I'll see you about daybreak then. We won't always go quite this long. But I wanted to get a good start on this new load, and besides, I wanted to see whether you'd turn out to be as good a man as you told me you was."

"How did I do?"

"Not bad. Not bad at all. By summer's end you could be a real help to me." He smiled, showing some missing teeth.

"I'll do my best." Joseph rubbed his aching hands against his legs. He wondered whether he would be able to unbend his fingers in the morning.

Joseph helped Brother Andrus gather up the axes and other tools, and they put them in the shed. There was no bed there, of course, but some straw was spread along one wall, where someone had apparently slept before. Joseph had no doubt he could sleep, but he suddenly realized he was going to miss his home more than he had expected.

Brother Andrus was about to leave, but he turned back and said, "You goin' up to call on that Engbert girl?"

Joseph felt his face get hot. "I might."

"I did some asking after you was here before. They tell me she's got a feller after her, calling on her twice a week."

Joseph tried to show no reaction. He nodded, then looked away. "Well, anyway, I'll see you in the morning."

"There's soap and a wash basin in the shed. You might even want to have yourself a good wash in the river and put on a fresh change of clothes. They say that feller that's been calling at the Engbert place slicks his hair down real nice and wears a good suit o' clothes. He's old enough to be your big brother — with about a dozen brothers and sisters in between."

Brother Andrus was still grinning, and he was watching for Joseph to react. "Maybe he can't chop as much wood in a day as I can," Joseph said.

"Now that's right. That's a good way to look at it." Brother Andrus slapped Joseph on the back, and then he walked away. Joseph could still hear him laughing when he was well up the path.

All the same, Joseph wasted no time in taking the advice he had gotten. He took a bar of soap to the river, stripped down, and walked out into the cold water. He washed as best he could and then put on the only change of clothes he had. Before long he was heading up Joseph Street again, this time wondering what he would say to explain his visit.

By the time he knocked on the door he could hear his own heart pounding. He wiped his wet palms on his shirt front. After a moment the door swung open and Brother Engbert looked out. "Yes?" he said.

"It's Joseph Williams, sir."

"Why so it is. My goodness, son, you've grown taller than I am. Step in. Step in. Mary Ann said you'd stopped by once."

Joseph stepped into the room and looked about. He saw Mary Ann quickly enough, but he also saw a man sitting next to her.

"Look at this, Malinda, David. You remember Joseph Williams, don't you?" They both came and shook Joseph's hand. Malinda, a little younger than Mary Ann, still wasn't much to look at, Joseph thought, but little David had grown considerably and was a nice-looking boy.

Sister Engbert stepped in from another room. She was wiping her hands on her apron. She looked rounder, healthier than Joseph remembered her. But then, he had known her during the terrible winter ordeal in Missouri. "Joseph, how nice to see you. What a handsome young man you've grown up to be."

Joseph glanced, ever so quickly, at Mary Ann, and saw her laugh. At the same time, he saw the man stand up. He was wearing a fine-looking suit. And then it struck Joseph who he must be. But this man was much too old for Mary Ann.

"Let me introduce you, Joseph. This is William Hall. He's fairly new to the Church. He came here last fall, almost as soon as he joined. He's from Pennsylvania."

Brother Hall held his hand out. "Very nice to meet you," he said, sounding quite formal. Joseph gave his hand a firm shake, even though his own hand was awfully sore from chopping wood.

"Joseph's family saved our lives," Sister Engbert said. "They took us into their home in Far West after we'd been starved out in DeWitt. They didn't have an awful lot to spare, but they shared everything they had with us."

"Joseph even tried to defend our lives once," Mary Ann said. She was still sitting down. Joseph took the chance to have a better look at her. She was wearing a yellow ribbon in her dark hair, and she was smiling, her dimples flashing. She had grown into a very pretty girl—prettier than he had expected, back in Missouri, and even prettier than she had looked in the garden a few weeks past. And then she added, "Of course, he wasn't much help against two grown men."

"He was a brave boy if he stood up to two men," Brother Hall said.

Joseph didn't reply. He was not happy with the word *boy,* nor with Mary Ann's little jab.

"Joseph, is your family here?" Brother Engbert asked.

"No. I've come on ahead. I plan to work this summer and raise a little cash. I'm also going to get a lot cleared and a house built so Mother and Ruth will have a place to move into. They plan to move here this fall."

"Where are you staying?"

"I've found a place for right now . . . near where I'm working."

"With a family?" Sister Engbert asked.

"Well, no. It's just a shed, really."

"That's hardly adequate," Brother Engbert said. "You'd be welcome to stay with us, of course, but I'm not sure you would find much comfort. Carla got married a while back and has moved out, but we got us a new little girl to take her place."

Joseph had noticed a baby and a little girl playing on the floor. The little girl, he realized, was Amy, the baby Sister Engbert had worried so much about two years before, when food had been so scarce. She looked healthy enough now. But Joseph could imagine that seven people must have filled the little cabin. There was more than one room—with a little side room, something of a lean-to in back, and a loft above—but the whole thing could have fit in a corner of the Hemsteads' house.

"You could certainly bed down in our barn until something better can be arranged."

"Thank you. I'm all right for now. I'll get something built on my own lot before long. It's not far from here."

"Well, all right," Sister Engbert said, "but plan on eating with us—every night if you like. Have you eaten tonight?"

"Well, no. But don't—"

"Sit down. Let me get you something."

Joseph nodded. It was what he had hoped for. And yet everything was changed from what he had imagined. This Brother Hall—this man—was sitting down next to Mary Ann again, as though he thought he belonged right by her side. Joseph could hardly think about anything else.

Joseph took a place at the table, across the room from Mary Ann. He talked to Brother Engbert about his family, but he kept watching Brother Hall, who was talking quietly with Mary

Ann. In a few minutes Sister Hall brought in a plate. "It's not much," she said. "A little pork and some greens. I wish I had known you were coming."

It looked good enough to Joseph. He began to eat, and he was suddenly aware how terribly hungry he was.

"What line of work are you in, young man?" Brother Hall asked. Joseph looked over and saw what pleasure Mary Ann had taken in the "young man."

"I've been running a farm down near Quincy," Joseph said.

"All by yourself, Joseph?" Mary Ann asked. "Whatever does your brother Matthew do?"

"Both of us have been running the farm."

"I see," Brother Hall said. "And what sort of work are you doing here?"

"For right now I'm chopping wood at the landing. It's just something to get me by."

"Oh, I know all about that," Brother Hall said. "A person has to take what he can get at times. I've had to take on pupils this last winter. I opened up a little school. And I'm a trained apothecary. I plan to open up my own shop when I can."

Joseph went back to his food. Who did this Hall think he was? A trained apothecary. A pompous old man is what he was. He was skinny as a fence post. He had no chest to speak of, no shoulders. His fingers looked like spider legs. How could Mary Ann sit with him like that? He was thirty years old if he was a day.

"Joseph," Mary Ann said, "you might think about going to Brother Hall's school this winter. Or have you finished school now?"

Joseph almost didn't answer. He saw Sister Engbert give Mary Ann a little shake of her head. Finally he said, "Finished some time ago," but he had taken enough. He would eat, and then he would get out. Mary Ann was pretty, but she had a tongue like a harpoon. She could marry this old fellow, for all Joseph cared.

"Well, now, Joseph," Brother Hall said, "you might give some thought to that." The man was not joking, as Mary Ann had been; he was quite serious. "I know that schooling tends to be hit-and-miss for most young people out here in the West. It never hurts to get all the education you can."

"That's right, Joseph," Mary Ann said. "You'll wish you had stayed in school longer—once you grow up to be a man."

Joseph pushed his plate back. He had gulped his food quickly and had thought that he could go for another plate or two. But he was not hungry now. "I better be going," he said to Brother Engbert, purposely avoiding Mary Ann as well as her friend.

Sister Engbert tried to get him to eat a little more, but Joseph thanked her and walked to the door. He stopped there, held his hat in his hand, thanked everyone, and stepped outside. Brother Engbert walked to the door, shook Joseph's hand, and wished him well. Sister Engbert stepped alongside and whispered, "Joseph, don't mind Mary Ann. She only means to tease you. She does that to all of us."

Joseph pretended not to have taken any offense. He thanked them again.

"Will you come back for supper tomorrow? I'll fix up something a little nicer?"

"I'm not sure I can make it," Joseph said. "But thanks anyway." He told himself, in fact, that he would never go near the place again, and he walked away.

He had only reached the gate, however, when he heard another voice, whispering. "Joseph, just a moment." He turned around and looked at Mary Ann, standing in the doorway with the door pulled mostly shut behind her. "I'm sorry," she said. "I really am. Will you come back tomorrow night?"

Joseph fumbled with the gate for a moment. He hardly knew his own mind. "No, thanks," he said, and was surprised by the anger in his own voice.

"Joseph, I really am sorry. I joke too much, and people don't know how to take me."

"Someone ought to take you over his knee, I'd say."

Mary Ann laughed, and then she pulled the door shut and took a few steps closer. "Will you please come back tomorrow night?" Joseph had lost his resolve, hearing her changed tone of voice, but he couldn't think what to say. "I don't like him at all, if that's what you think."

"Who's that?"

"Joseph, you know what I mean. Come back tomorrow night, all right?"

"All right."

"Good. I'll see you then." She smiled, looking delighted, and then she turned and hurried back to the house.

Later that night, lying on the hard ground in the little shed, it occurred to Joseph that he didn't remember walking back to the wood yard. Somehow he had gotten there, but it must have all happened in a haze. Or maybe he tripped and fell all the way back in a single leap. It was just as likely.

Chapter 9

Early in July, Ruth fell ill. She woke up one morning confused and hot, her head buzzing with pain. It was very early and still quite dark in the room. She instinctively reached for her mother, who was next to her in the bed. "Mother," she whispered.

Sister Williams seemed to know from Ruth's voice. She turned and touched her face. "Oh, dear," she said, "you're burning up." She sat up and hesitated for just a moment. Then Ruth heard her whisper, "Please don't let this happen."

Ruth knew what she meant. Summer fevers were a source of terror to every family. This year, up and down the Mississippi river valley—not just in Nauvoo—the ague had taken all too many lives. And there was not much anyone could do. Just wait.

For the next few days Ruth hardly knew the difference between consciousness and the strange dreams that flowed through her mind. All the same, she was aware of her mother, or sometimes one of the Hemsteads, by her side, washing her face and arms with cool cloths or just sitting by her. Ruth knew, abstractly, that they feared for her life. But she never felt the fear. She knew where she was, even in all the chaos of her dreams, and she was not going to give up. Father had died of a fever; so had little Samuel. But Ruth would not. She would not accept such a stupid end to her life.

After a week she was beginning to be more coherent. She awoke one afternoon to find Mr. Hemstead sitting by her bed.

She could see more clearly than she had since before the illness had begun.

"Hello, little one," he said. "I like that look in your eye. You can see me, can't you?"

"Yes," Ruth said, her voice hardly a whisper.

"Come now. You can speak up better than that. You've been talking plenty the last two hours."

"What did I say?" Ruth asked, somehow aware that she had been talking, but not sure about what.

"Well, all kinds of things. But you kept saying that you're not going to live in that mud hole, Nauvoo. That's what made me laugh."

Ruth felt herself smile a little although she hardly had the energy to stay awake.

"I want you to drink a little water," Mr. Hemstead said. He reached under Ruth's shoulders and brought her up to the glass he held. "You hardly weigh anything at all, little one. But you can start eating now. You'll get your strength back in time. At least the fever is breaking."

Ruth slept again. She didn't know how long, but when she awoke Mr. Hemstead was still there. He was watching her. She could see his white hair, the droopy mustache; but she also knew that peaceful look of his, when he was feeling good about things. His forehead had smoothed out, and the wrinkles around his eyes had disappeared.

"Your mother's getting some broth ready for you. She'll bring it up soon and we'll give you a little. You'll have to take your time and rest easy, but I know you're going to be all right now."

"Did you think I was going to die?"

"Well, let's say that I worried about you there for a few days."

"I knew I wouldn't die."

"Oh, is that right? And how did you know?"

"Because it made me mad to think of it. I don't want to die. I hate death."

Mr. Hemstead laughed quietly. His laugh was always just a

gentle rumble in his throat. "I'm not too much in love with the idea myself," he said.

"You're not old enough to die."

"Oh, we're all old enough. But not many of us ever think we are."

Ruth looked at the pretty wallpaper across the room. For so many days she had not been able to focus on anything very far away. Now the small print—the pineapples and the strings of flowers—were all clear to her. She thought she would like to get up soon.

"I told your mother that I thought you should all stay on here a little longer. Maybe another year. You're going to be weak for quite some time. That 'mud hole' wouldn't do you any good." He laughed.

"What did Mother say?"

"Very little. Well, she did say that people can get sick here, too, and she pointed at you as proof. I can't argue with that. All the same, I think you're better off here this winter than you would be in a drafty cabin."

"What does Matthew say?"

"I don't know. I haven't talked to him about it. But I know he would rather stay."

"Do we have to go just because Mother wants to?"

"Well, little one, I would never try to create problems between you and your mother. What she thinks—and what Matthew agrees to—I'll just have to accept." Mr. Hemstead suddenly sat up straighter, as though another thought had struck him. "Ruth, if you would like to stay on, at least for a time, you would always be welcome."

"Mother wouldn't let me."

"I'm not so sure. She's been awfully worried about you these last few days. And you know how Matthew feels. They might be willing to let you stay on for a time—maybe a year or two. You could go to school, and we would treat you like our very own."

"That would be nice, Mr. Hemstead." Ruth's mind was still in a whir; yet she knew what she was doing, and she didn't like it. She felt the way she had the day she sneaked the dress out of the house.

"Ruth, you will always have a place with us. If you do leave, you could come back someday, if you like. When you're older. If your brothers won't stay and take the farm, you could marry and bring your husband here. I would give the whole place to you. All I would ask is that we could stay here in our old age. You might have to look out for us a little, but we're not ones to need much attention."

"You're too kind to me, Mr. Hemstead," Ruth said.

"Oh, no. Oh, no. I'm too selfish, that's what I am."

"Selfish?"

"I lost my only little girl." He sat for a time. "I raised sons after that, and I thought they would want this place. And one after the other they each decided to move on somewhere. Not one of them wanted to settle here. So I cling to your brothers and to you. It's a terrible thing to grow old alone. And it's a terrible thing to work your whole life for something and then just see it all lost."

Neither said anything for a time, and then Ruth heard that little, deep rumble of a laugh. "You may hate death, little one, but not as much as I do."

"I'll stay, Mr. Hemstead. I will if they'll let me. And if they won't, maybe I can come back someday."

Mr. Hemstead winked, and looked very pleased. He seemed to be getting ready to say something else when Mother came into the room. "Is anyone around here hungry?" she said.

Ruth was not hungry, but she did want energy. If she could get it quickly, she would drink all the broth her mother could bring her.

Mother helped Ruth sit up a little. Mr. Hemstead fluffed up the down pillow and placed it under Ruth's shoulders and head. "She's going to be all right," he told Mother, and then he left the room.

Mother began to spoon the broth into Ruth's mouth. After a time, she said, "Now don't take too much all at once. Let's wait just a little and see how your stomach accepts it." She was

talking in a kindly tone, one that Ruth remembered but hadn't
heard much lately. "I heard you and Mr. Hemstead talking up
here. What was he saying to you?"

"He told me about his own little daughter and his sons."

"Really? What did he tell you about them?"

"Nothing. Just that he misses them. He doesn't want to get
old by himself."

Ruth saw the reaction, the twinge. "Ruth, I know he wants
us to stay. But we must consider lots of things. We have our
own responsibilities."

"I know."

"Ruth, I don't know whether you do know. It's so very hard
for you to understand. Right now, at your age, it's not easy for
you to see why moving on to Nauvoo is so important."

"Matthew is older. He doesn't understand, either."

"Well, that isn't exactly true. I think he understands. But
he has always wanted his own farm. He's wanted a place like
this. It's not easy for him to turn his back on it."

Mother was looking closely at Ruth. She put her hand on
her forehead. "But let's not talk about that now. You need your
rest. We may decide to stay on a little longer now. We're not
about to move you until you're back to your full health. But I
do want you to know that one of the main reasons I want to
rejoin the Saints is for your sake. I love you, and I want the
best for you."

Ruth liked the touch of her mother's arm around her shoulders, liked the softness in her voice. But the talk of leaving still
scared her. "Mr. Hemstead said I could stay here, if I wanted.
He said that if you moved on to Nauvoo, I could stay—away
from all the sickness—and I could go to school." She thought
about telling the rest, about inheriting the farm, but she could
see that Mother was not reacting well to what she had already
said.

"Ruth, Mr. Hemstead had no right to . . . ." Mother stopped
and took a breath. "Mr. Hemstead loves you, Ruth, and he's
been very kind to all of us. I know he wouldn't purposely set

out to break up our family. But in his love for you, he forgets that I have to decide what's best."

"He said that. But he thinks that you — and Matthew — might think it's best for me to stay on for a time."

"Ruth, are you that willing to let us go without you?"

That was not it. That was not fair. She had not really thought what it would mean to have Mother and Matthew leave her. She didn't want that. And she missed Joseph. All the same, she knew that it wasn't fair to be forced to go someplace she didn't want to go. Mother would never understand that.

"Ruth, honey, we never should have started to talk about this now. You don't need any agitation. You need to rest, and to eat, and to get your strength back."

Ruth let herself relax in the comfort of her mother's care. She couldn't settle all this now — and she liked feeling loved. If only her choices were not so terrible. If only things could be simpler. She slipped back to sleep, resting against her mother's softness.

Chapter 10

Joseph's summer was difficult. He had imagined himself working to build the kingdom. He thought he would like that better than plowing Mr. Hemstead's fields. But chopping wood was just plain hard work, kingdom or not.

He did feel good about the lot he had chosen. It was relatively high, not wet at all, and covered with small oaks and cottonwood trees. Clearing the land was hard work, but some of the oaks were large enough to provide logs for the house.

Joseph found the going very slow. Brother Andrus expected a man to put in a full day. Demand for wood to burn on the riverboats was constant. Joseph was also called to the landing at times to help load cargo. By the time he got to his own work he was always tired. He found himself longing for sunset just as he had done all spring. But he was making progress. The clearing was coming to an end. Preparing logs would go faster.

Sunset came late, however, and Joseph's days stretched long. The underbrush was gradually disappearing, and the logs were piling up, but he had planned a large house, had promised something very fine, and he knew he would have to keep his promise or disappoint Mother and Matthew and especially Ruth.

The best part of each day was that the Engberts always welcomed him for supper. That meant he got a chance to see Mary Ann almost every day. The family was always there, however, and Joseph had to leave soon after eating so he could get back to his work. Some nights Brother Hall would come around, and no matter what Mary Ann had said about him, he acted like he owned the girl. He would reach out and pat her hand or whisper to her. Joseph felt like knocking him down when he did that, or at least telling him to keep his hands to himself.

But he and Mary Ann had no understanding. Other than the time she had told him that she didn't like Brother Hall, they had hardly said anything personal to each other at all. And in spite of her apologies that night, she still liked to tease.

"Joseph, do you think someday you'll be one of the greatest woodchoppers this world has ever known?" she asked him one night at supper. When Joseph refused to answer, she added, "By the way, who are some of the world's great woodchoppers? One never hears much about them."

"Paul Bunyan's probably about the best," Brother Engbert said, and everyone laughed, including Joseph. But in truth, he could have lived without some of Mary Ann's little jabs.

During the day Joseph was seeing a world he had never known. He saw the daily parade of fancy boats on the river, and he saw the people who traveled on them. He had traveled down the Missouri once himself, but the Mississippi riverboats were much finer, much bigger than the ones he had seen.

And he also saw the riffraff that moved in and out of Nauvoo, the ones Brother Andrus had warned him about. Joseph slept with a rifle at night, and he heard people coming and going outside the shed, jumping out of skiffs and talking about their exploits. He suspected that some were thieves, that they were crossing the river by night and raiding river towns. He had sometimes stepped outside to see what he could, but he saw very little in the dark.

One day, early in the afternoon, as the damp heat was reaching the unbearable point, Joseph was called to the landing to help the roustabouts unload cargo from a big riverboat. The load included pelts for a local tanner, but the skins had not been treated and the stench was sickening. He had to throw big bundles up on his back and haul them to the makeshift dock,

then heft them up onto a wagon. He wondered whether he
would ever wash the smell from his shirt.

When he unloaded the last of the pelts, Joseph stood on
the dock for a moment. There was a bit of air moving, and he
hoped it would cool his sweating body. The heat was too intense,
however, and the breeze too slight. He could hardly stand the
thought of returning to the wood yard to pick up his ax again.
His hands were hardened now, not oozing with blisters as they
had been early in the summer, but his back never seemed to
get enough rest to recover.

All the same, he would have to go back. Work was not easy
to find in Nauvoo, and he knew of nothing better that he could
do.

"Hello there."

Joseph looked up toward the boat. He saw a man on the
promenade deck, up high. He was wearing a fancy brocade
waistcoat with a gold chain hanging from his watch pocket. He
was smoking a long cigar.

"Yes, you. Step up here a moment and catch a little air. I
want to talk to you."

"Sorry. I've got to get along now." Joseph wanted nothing
to do with such men.

"Come up. It will be worth your while."

Joseph had heard stories of rich men asking for some trivial
bit of help with a trunk or some baggage and then dropping a
gold piece into the hand of the roustabout. Maybe this was not
a chance to pass up. Joseph hesitated, but he decided to satisfy
his curiosity. He crossed onto the boat and hiked up the stairs
to the promenade deck.

As Joseph approached, the man grinned. "How do you like
that work?" he said.

Joseph smiled. "It's honest," he said.

"Yes, yes. Exactly. I've always noticed, the more honest the
work, the lower the pay. Strange thing, isn't it?" He held his
hand out. Joseph shook it. "The name's Holley — George Holley.
Or at least it is today. Names have a way of slipping away from
me, but I always find a new one."

Joseph knew this was anything but a decent man, but he suspected he might be quite entertaining—had Joseph time for such things. "You seem to have found something that pays better," Joseph said. "Are you telling me that it isn't honest?"

"Let's put it this way. I tried honesty for a number of years, but never did eat well, let alone dress the way I like. Dishonesty suits me better, if you take my meaning." He gestured at his clothes.

"I'll stand downwind," Joseph said. "The smell of some of my honesty might blow off on you." But Joseph had no time to banter with the man. "Is there something I can do for you?"

"Yes. I would like to be rich, not just comfortable. And I might as well make you comfortable in the process. How does that sound to you?"

"I think I'd rather tote hides than get my own hide skinned. You already warned me what kind of man you are."

"Very good. Fine answer. You're a clever boy. Just exactly what I'm looking for. You have a face any mother would love and all that pretty, straw-colored hair. And yet you've got a sharp eye. That's what I need."

"Sir, I'm not—"

"All right. Now listen to me for one minute. I'll be direct." The man held the cigar with all four fingers, took a deep draw on it. "I play cards. I win. And the reason I win is that I improve my odds. The best way to do that is to work with a partner. And the best partner is an innocent looking boy who can walk behind a man without attracting much attention, but a boy who can spot every card in a man's hand at a quick glance. A few little signals after that, and I'm a richer man. And so would you be."

"No, thanks," Joseph said.

"Just think of this, young man. In one day you can make as much as you might make in a year rousting these boats. In one trip up and down this river you could set yourself up in some little business—a farm or a mill—or whatever it is you dream about when you're totin' those stinking skins and barrels of whiskey."

The man was good. He was making Joseph feel the irony

of it all. Joseph had certainly done his dreaming out there in
the wood yard. He'd thought of striking gold and setting himself
up in business. Banking would be in Joseph's line, he thought.
He had seen those bankers walk along the streets of Quincy,
decked out in a nice suit of clothes and seeming to own the
town.

"No thanks, sir. I need to get back to work." Joseph's disappointment was greater than he had suspected. He had hoped
at least for a half dollar, earned without much effort.

"So you'll take your reward in heaven?"

"Yes, sir."

"Well, I'm a man who plays the odds. I'm betting there is
no heaven. I'm betting that we die and the worms eat us. If I'm
right, you surely are wasting a chance here."

"What if you're wrong?"

The man took a puff on his cigar and blew the smoke into
the air. "Do I look worried?"

He didn't. Joseph had to admit that. As he returned to the
dock, he heard the man laugh and yell good-bye. But Joseph
didn't look up. He headed away to the wood yard.

"Hey. Fellow."

Joseph looked around and saw a man he had seen before
but had never met. He was often around the landing.

"What did that gambler want?" the man asked.

Joseph was a little ashamed he had even listened. He didn't
want to say much. "He's not up to any good."

"What did he say to you?"

"He said he needed a partner. Someone who could help
him cheat."

"That's what I thought. A lot of those men take on young
fellows to eagle-eye for them."

Joseph nodded. He was about to turn away.

"Why didn't you take him up on it?"

"I guess I didn't like the odds," Joseph said.

"Maybe you made a mistake."

Joseph couldn't understand the man's tone. He seemed to
mean it.

"Don't look so surprised. A lot of Mormons feel like they got a little coming back after all that's been stripped away from 'em."

"Are you a Mormon?"

"Of course. Don't I look righteous? I only just found the true light of the gospel not so long ago." He was grinning as though he had told a wonderful joke. He only had about half his teeth.

"You don't really justify thieving?"

"Oh, but I do. And if you see me crossing the river some night, don't think it's because I like to do a little sight-seeing down on the Missouri side of the river."

Joseph stared at the man, tried to get some hint as to whether he was serious. "We've had our Danites, Brother," Joseph said. "Look what Avard and his kind did to the Church. We don't need any more of that."

"Well, I don't know much about that, 'cept what Alonson Brown tells me. He says religion ain't just walking around with a sweet face; it's doing what's right. And sometimes that means *making* things right."

Joseph had heard the talk, heard that certain of the Saints felt this way. But he had never come face to face with it. "A thief is a thief, Brother. Alonson Brown is accused of stealing; and if that's what he's been doing, he's no better than that thief up there on the riverboat. They both have a spot waiting for them in hell."

Joseph walked away, but he heard the man laugh and say, "Brother Brown just collected a few offerings from the good people of Missouri, that's all."

Joseph chopped wood the rest of the afternoon, but when he left the wood yard that day he went straight to Joseph Smith's log house. Emma Smith answered the door. She had her new little baby in her arms. "I'm sorry to bother you, Sister Smith," Joseph said, "but I need to talk to Brother Joseph if he has just a minute or two. It's quite important."

"Surely. Come in," she said. Joseph knew Sister Smith fairly well, but he always felt a little self-conscious around her. She had a certain refinement that made him feel very much the backwoods boy.

As Joseph stepped through the door he suddenly noticed his own smell. He could see that she noticed it, too. "I'm sorry," he said. "I was hauling pelts this afternoon."

"You smell like hard work," she said, and she smiled. "That never was an offense to me."

"Thank you," Joseph said, and then he followed her to the Prophet's room, the place he used as an office.

Brother Joseph always seemed happy to be interrupted, whether he really was or not. "Come in. Come in," he said.

"Brother Joseph, I won't take a minute." Joseph then rehearsed the whole story, telling every word the man at the landing had said.

Brother Joseph didn't look surprised, and when the story was told, he said, "I know about this, Joseph. You're not the first to come to me."

"What can we do? Men like that will destroy the Church." Joseph was more than frustrated; he was angry.

Brother Joseph nodded. "It's worse than you know. Brown and some others were captured and hauled off to Missouri, and they were beaten up pretty bad. I thought they were victims. I listened to their story and took them at their word. Brown and his men told me that someone had stashed goods along the bank and then blamed them, just to make us Mormons look bad. I believed that. But now it turns out that a whole lot more was stashed than anyone would ever think to carry across the river just to set a trap."

"What will you do now?"

"I don't know. We can't win. I guess Brown will get what's coming to him. But all of us will pay a price."

"Why can't things ever just go . . . a little easier, Brother Joseph?"

The Prophet smiled. "I've asked that question a few times myself. A little less sickness would be a fine thing for Nauvoo. A little less death. And a little more money to pay our debts.

Most of all, a little more righteousness. That would help as much as anything."

Joseph thought so too. Why was it that when he peeled away the surface of things, what lay beneath was never so pure and good as he wanted it to be?

"Joseph, are you still sleeping in the shed at the wood yard?"

"Yes. I keep planning to find something better, but there's never any time left in my day."

"Well, it's just as well. Watch what's happening around there. We've got to police ourselves. We can't trust that a man's heart is right just because he asks to be baptized."

"All right. I'll watch," Joseph said. But he wanted to do much more than that. He wanted to catch such men. He wanted to kick their backsides for them. He wanted to stop them from destroying the kingdom he was trying to build.

Chapter 11

That night Joseph decided to have a better look around. He had heard men downriver some nights. If they had made a cache of their stolen goods, it was probably not far away. Joseph waited until after dark, and then he slipped out of the shed. He took Brother Andrus's rifle along.

The moon was close to full, but a thin layer of clouds kept the night quite dark. Joseph walked along the banks of the river and then moved back into the woods in places that looked convenient for unloading a skiff.

But he found nothing. Under the trees everything was so dark that he had little hope of seeing much. He would do better in the day, of course, but he could also be spotted very easily.

He moved down the bank maybe a quarter of a mile, and by then he knew he was farther down the river than the men usually came ashore. He started back. Coming the other way, he noticed a spot where the grass had been trampled into a trail into the trees. He decided to walk back in just a little ways.

That's when he took a step or two into the darkness, tried to see, and then realized the woods were too dense. He couldn't even see where the trail led. And then he heard a voice: "All right. Stop right there. I've got a gun pointed at you."

Joseph jumped back instinctively, then ran. He heard a pop, and a bullet buzzed by him. He turned to run up the shore when a second bullet whizzed through the dark. Suddenly, without thinking, he dove toward the water, where he could get down and out of sight.

The water was not more than a foot deep. He had dropped into a weed-filled swamp several feet from the current of the river. He heard a voice behind him. "He jumped in the river. Out that way some'eres."

Joseph didn't dare move. The men could see better out here away from the woods. They would not shoot quite so wildly. But maybe they wouldn't spot him if he stayed quiet. Maybe they would think he had gotten out into the river and was downstream by now.

Joseph held his breath as long as he could and tried not to move at all. He was lying on his side, only partly under water. He still had the rifle, but it was only a single-shot; he would never have a chance to reload if he did get off a shot.

"He must be swimming for it," one of the men said. They were behind Joseph. He couldn't see them.

"I don't think so. I never saw anythin' on the water. You sure he jumped in?"

"Yup. I heard him."

"Then he must be layin' down out here in these reeds some'ere."

Joseph heard the man's voice come a little closer. He knew he had to do something. He needed to get underwater. He could move suddenly, startle them, and try to throw himself into deeper water, but he knew the first time his head came up he would be dead. Then he felt the rifle barrel alongside his face. He slowly moved the barrel to his mouth. He sucked to make sure that air would pass through the chamber, and then slowly he pulled his legs up toward his chest.

"Look, them reeds is moving."

Joseph suddenly drove his legs, rising up and then flipping backwards, like a sea animal. When he hit the deeper water he kept his mouth on the gun barrel and sucked for air. The butt of the rifle was in the air, but he was underwater, pushing himself downstream with his feet. He heard the crash of a bullet, drove his legs hard again, and kept himself underwater by pushing with his heels. He kept moving downstream that way as long as he could, and then he sucked and got water; he had let the gun

get too deep. He spun and let go of the rifle, swam hard under
water for a few strokes, and then gasped as he hit the surface.

"There he is. Way down river."

Another bullet struck the water nearby, but now Joseph was
well into the current, flowing downstream. He was soon out of
sight. All the same, he kept swimming and got himself far beyond
the distance the men might run in the same time, and then he
headed for shore. He pulled himself into another bog and lay
there, gasping. He knew he couldn't wait long. He doubted the
men would try to come that far down the bank, with all the
swamps and rocky outcroppings, but he wasn't about to wait
around to make sure.

He pulled himself up and then headed into the dark woods
nearby. Here in the dark he rested again and tried to think
what he should do. He could circle around through town and
come back to the shed, but he didn't know if the men had
recognized him or not. It was doubtful, but he thought it would
be safer to go somewhere else. He decided to try to get to the
Engberts, who lived well away from the river.

It was dark but not late. Joseph saw lantern light in many
of the cabins as he walked through town. He stayed away from
any people he saw, however, He didn't want to answer questions
about being so wet and muddy.

When he got to the Engberts, he wondered whether anyone
was still up. The night was hot, but the windows and doors were
closed to keep the mosquitoes and other night insects out. Joseph stepped to the door and knocked anyway, and then he
stepped back where he would be mostly in the dark.

Brother Engbert came to the door. "Joseph, is that you?"

"Yes, sir. I was wondering if I could sleep in your barn."

"Well, sure. You could come in and—"

"No, that's quite all right. I just didn't want you to hear me
and think I was some stranger. I'll just say goodnight now,
and—"

"Joseph, is something the matter?"

"No, not at all. I just needed a place to sleep tonight."

Joseph was not entirely sure why he didn't want to explain, but he did know that he was hoping not to see Mary Ann at all.

"Don't you need a blanket, or—"

"No, no. It's a hot night. I'll be just fine."

And so Joseph went to the barn. He climbed into the loft and found a place in the hay where he could lie down. But already he wished he had taken a blanket. His clothes were mucky and uncomfortable.

He was wide awake anyway, and he knew he wouldn't be able to settle down and sleep very easily. He wondered who the men were who had tried to kill him. He hadn't seen either of them. He supposed that he had walked almost on top of them where they were sleeping in the woods. But he also knew that they had no reason to be shooting at anyone unless they had something to hide.

An hour must have gone by, and Joseph was not any closer to going to sleep. There were mosquitoes in the barn, and they had found him. Joseph slapped at them as they buzzed by his ear. He could feel that he already had a number of bites. His clothes would not dry in the humid air, either, which left him feeling damp.

And then he heard someone struggling with the latch on the barn door. Had the men somehow followed him all this way? Joseph lay still, listening carefully, trying to think what he should do.

"Joseph?"

It was Mary Ann. What did she want?

"Joseph, where are you?"

"In the loft."

"I thought you might want a blanket."

"Fine. Leave it there. I'll come down and get it when you're gone."

She was holding a coal-oil lamp, which she raised now. She was looking up toward the loft, the lamp illuminating her smile. "Don't you have your clothes on?" she asked, looking impish.

"Yes, I do."

"Well, then, what are you so worried about? Come down for a minute. I want to talk to you."

"Does your father know you're out here?"

"Of course not. It's not proper."

"That's right. It isn't."

"Since when did you become so strict?"

"I'm not strict. I just don't think you should be out here this time of night—with me here."

She was looking at him curiously, holding the lamp as high as she could. "Why is your hair all matted down, and what's that on your face?"

"Look, it's a long story. I'll tell you about it another time."

"Come on, Joseph, this is the first exciting thing that has happened to me for a long time. Don't send me away."

"Exciting? What's so exciting?"

"You sleeping in my barn, of course—and acting mysterious. Come down, all right? Tell me what's going on."

"All right. But I don't need you laughing at me. You find enough excuses for that." Joseph slid over onto the ladder and climbed down.

"Joseph, you're all wet," she said, as he made his way down. "You look like some poor little puppy that got himself caught in the rain."

"You said you wouldn't laugh at me."

"I never keep promises. You should know that by now."

"Yes, I should." Joseph sounded a little more serious than he really meant to.

"Actually, I do. But some promises are a little hard to keep. And you do look funny."

Joseph ran his fingers through his hair. Mary Ann looked pretty, he thought. Her hair was combed out and was picking up glints from the lamp; her eyes were catching the light, too. He was glad she had come out, even if he did look so bad.

"Now tell me what happened."

Joseph did. He saw no good place to sit down, so he just stood in front of her and told his story, going all the way back to the gambler on the riverboat and his talk with Joseph Smith.

"You thought fast, Joseph," she said when he was finished. "I'm glad you did. I'm glad you're not out there in the Mississippi floating face down on your way to New Orleans."

"That's not so funny. I almost was."

"I didn't say it was funny."

"You make everything sound funny. You laugh at just about everything I do."

"I can't help that. That's just how I am. Do you want to marry me?"

"What?" Joseph really wasn't sure he had heard right.

"I can't stand out here much longer. And I need to know."

"Mary Ann, I can't just—"

"Yes, you can. And you better speak up soon. Brother Hall wants to marry me. My parents say that I should say yes just as soon as he asks straight out."

"Mary Ann, he's way too old for you."

"Father doesn't think so. He says he has both feet on the ground."

"Well, he needs to plant them in the ground, or he'll blow away with the first good wind."

Mary Ann laughed. "That's all well and good, but at least he's not afraid to make his intentions clear."

Joseph felt something grab inside him, but he didn't know what to say. He just stood there looking at her.

Mary Ann set the lantern down, and her eyes softened in the dim light. "What should I tell him, Joseph?"

"Don't marry him, Mary Ann. Please don't."

"Why?"

"You know why."

"Why, Joseph? Tell me."

"Because I want to marry you."

"Why?"

"Mary Ann, don't—"

"Joseph, tell me why you want to marry me. I want to hear it."

"Because I love you." He couldn't look at her.

Suddenly she grabbed him around the neck and kissed him

hard, but not very long. And then she stepped aside, grabbed the lantern, and headed for the door. "Don't make me wait too long, Joseph. All right?"

"Mary Ann, I don't know when I can get married. I have to build a house for my family, and then I'll have to—"

"Just don't make me wait too long. My parents will try to make me marry Brother Hall. And I don't want to marry him. I want to marry you. But I can't wait forever." And then she was gone.

Joseph was standing in the dark, not knowing whether to jump in the air and shout for joy, or to sit down and cry. One idea seemed about as good as the other, but he did neither. He took the blanket back up to the loft and lay down on it, but he slept not one minute all night. He was trying to think how he could manage it all. And he was thinking about Mary Ann. He kept hoping that she was awake, too, just a few yards away in the house; and he hoped she was thinking about him.

Chapter 12

As Ruth approached the little white schoolhouse, she looked about at the students who were outside. She told herself she was looking for Emmie. A group of younger children were out in front, playing, dashing about. Ruth knew they were excited about the first day of school. She also saw a group of older boys assembled in their usual spot. But she didn't see one particular boy. She wondered if he would come back. Not many boys continued coming to school much past fourteen or fifteen.

"Ruth." Ruth turned around to see Emmie coming up behind her. "Didn't you hear me calling? I've been trying to catch up to you."

"I'm sorry."

"You never looked back for me, not even once. That's because you were staring at those boys, trying to see Justin."

"Don't be silly. I was looking for you. I thought you would be ahead of me."

"Oh, Ruth, it's so good to see you! I've missed you so much." Emmie threw her arms around Ruth. The girls had not seen each other all summer, not since the day Ruth had been caught in her lie. "Are you feeling all right now?"

"Yes. I'm good as new."

"But you were very sick, weren't you? My mother heard that you came near dying."

"That's what my mother thinks, but I don't. I never gave it a serious thought."

Emmie laughed. "Oh, Ruth, that's how you are. You know your own mind. You'll find a prince to marry someday, and then you'll tell him what's what in the palace."

Somehow their old talk of princes and palaces seemed childish now. "Emmie, I'm afraid I don't see any princes around here."

"Not only that, your prince is not coming back to school. His father says he has to stay and help on the farm this fall, at least until the harvest is over."

"After the harvest we'll be moving on. We're moving to Nauvoo."

Emmie stopped. Ruth continued ahead a few steps before she looked back. "Ruth, don't tell me that. I can't bear to think it."

"I know. I can't either."

"Can't you do anything?"

Ruth started to walk again, and Emmie caught up. "Mr. Hemstead would like to have me stay. He's told my mother that I should stay on for a time, to make sure my health has really returned. But Mother says I'll be fine."

"She's going to make you move?"

"I think so. Matthew could be convinced, I think, but when I try to talk to him about it, he just says, 'That's for Mother to decide.' "

"Oh, Ruth, that's awful!" The two were at the school now. They stopped near the little step by the front door. "You'll never meet your prince now. It will be the saddest story I ever heard. You'll be like a lady in a sad, sad story I read. You'll move to that ugly little town and you'll pine away without your love, and then you'll fall sick and die, and I'll never see you again."

"Emmie!"

"Well, how do you think I feel, losing my best friend this way? Have a little pity on me." Emmie laughed.

"Fine. But don't kill me off in the first chapter of this sad story of yours." Ruth laughed, too, but somehow Emmie's sort of humor was not so funny as it once had been.

The two went inside and sat down. Miss Gordon was over-joyed to see them. She hugged them both and said she knew they were going to be two of her best girls. And to Ruth she said, "You're one of the best scholars ever. I expect big things from you this year."

"Never mind that," Emmie said. "She's going off to—"

"Emmie, never mind," Ruth said.

School seemed slow to Ruth that day. Knowing that she wouldn't be there more than a month or two made the whole thing seem sort of pointless. At lunchtime, however, Emmie hurried to Ruth and said, "We have to talk. I have a plan."

"I remember the last time you had a plan. It got me in a whole lot of trouble."

"This is a better one."

The girls went outside, took their lunches, and sat in the shade of a clump of sumac, far from the school. "First of all, there's something you need to know. Maybe I shouldn't tell you, because it might break your heart, but I have to tell you anyway."

"Break my heart?"

"Yes. If you leave, you will never see Justin again. But you need to know, he loves you desperately."

"Emmie, please. Don't start that again."

"Oh, but it's true. I saw him almost every Sunday all summer. And one day he walked up to me and asked me right out whether it was true that you were sick. He even said, 'I heard she was very sick.' "

"Emmie, that's just—"

"Ruth, no boy would dare to ask about a girl unless he loved her very much. It would be too embarrassing. And listen to this. He said, 'If you see her, tell her I hope she gets better soon.' "

"My goodness, that is a declaration of love."

"Don't make fun, Ruth. You didn't see his face. He looked like a loon sounds when you think it's out there dying for love, but just sounds like that."

"What?"

"He looked sick, Ruth. He looked worried almost to tears.

He thought you were dying and he would never hold you in his arms. Never kiss your cherry red lips."

Ruth laughed and shook her head, and Emmie laughed a little, too, but she quickly added, "It's all true. But think of it: if you leave, it's the same as dying, even if you don't die. He'll probably fall ill and die himself. I've read about things like that. And if he sees you now, more beautiful than ever, so delicate after your illness, he'll probably never make it through the first winter."

"Emmie, I know this is all stuff for a novel for you. But it's worse for me. I don't think it's anything to joke about. I don't want to leave."

"Joke? Is that what you think? You think I'm joking? On the saddest day of my life, you think I'm joking?"

"Emmie, you're turning it into one of your love stories, the way you always do. But for me it means moving, giving up my home, and losing Miss Gordon."

"And it's losing Justin, too. Tell the truth. You do like him?"

"Emmie, I'm only twelve. How can I 'lose' someone when I'm twelve years old?"

"He's about to be fifteen—that's how. He's almost grown. He knows that, and he's picked you out to be his wife."

Ruth decided not to talk any more on the subject. The truth was, she did think Justin was the nicest and best-looking boy she knew. But to think about being "chosen" by him someday was much more complicated than Emmie would ever understand.

"Ruth, don't worry. I have a good plan, and you can start today. When you get home from school—during supper—just look tired and hang your head a little. Then go to bed early. And when the Hemsteads or your mother ask you how you're doing, say, 'Oh, fine. I'm just fine.' "

"What will that do, Emmie?" But Ruth understood.

"They'll all worry about you. They'll say that you still don't have your strength back, that you might be having a relapse."

"Mother says Joseph is building us a good house in Nauvoo, and I'll be just as well off there as I am here."

"That's what she tells you, but she has to have some doubts, especially with Matthew and the Hemsteads more worried about it than she is. They'll say something to her. They'll make her feel that she isn't a good mother if she drags you up there."

"Emmie, I don't want to lie to my mother again. I didn't feel good about it last time."

"Ruth, we were much younger then, and we made a terrible mistake. The note was wrong. I admit it. But this is different. You won't lie. You'll always say you feel fine, or maybe if you really are tired, you can say so."

"Emmie, if I'm moping around and hanging my head when I feel fine, I'm lying. Can't you see that?"

"No, I can't. There's a difference."

"What difference?"

"I'm not exactly sure. But you're not really lying unless you *say* something untrue." She thought for a moment. "It's not bearing false witness; that's what the Bible says you shouldn't do. I'm pretty sure you have to say something to bear false witness."

"Emmie, you know as well as I do that it's deceiving, the same as we did with the note."

"No. I think it's not so bad. And besides, God will probably forgive you for it since you're only trying to save your life."

"Emmie, I don't know whether or not I want to stay with the Hemsteads if my family leaves."

"But the Hemsteads would treat you like a queen. They would buy you everything—and they would let you visit me any time you wanted."

"But they're not my family, Emmie. Would you want to live without your family?"

"With Mr. Hemstead showering me with all kinds of—"

"Emmie, I'm serious. I'm talking about real life. Wouldn't you miss your mother?"

Emmie took a long look at Ruth. "I guess so," she finally said. "But won't they all stay if they think it would be bad for you to go?"

"Maybe. Mother's worried about more than my health,

though. She thinks we should be with the members of our church."

"Oh, Ruth. That's crazy."

"Emmie, don't say that." Ruth got to her feet. "Do you hear me? Don't ever say that again."

"I'm sorry. I didn't mean—"

"I know what you meant." Ruth walked back to the school. And all afternoon she fumed when she thought of Emmie. But that night, at supper, Ruth felt wilted. Maybe it was the heat and the long walk. She had not gotten out a great deal since her illness.

"Little one, are you all right?" Mr. Hemstead asked.

"Yes, I'm fine," she answered, and immediately she wondered whether she had been hanging her head on purpose.

"You do look tired," Ruth's mother said. "You should go to bed early tonight. I don't think you have all your strength back yet."

"I'm fine, Mother." Ruth tried to raise her head and look as strong as possible. But when she tried to clear the table, her mother sent her upstairs to rest.

So she did go upstairs and sit between the window and the door, where she could feel a little air moving through. She could hear the others talking downstairs.

"Elizabeth," Mrs. Hemstead said, "I worry about you taking her away this fall."

"Most of the sickness comes in the summer."

"Yes, but she's grown accustomed to this nice, warm house," Mr. Hemstead said. "I'm not so sure that a cold little cabin will be good for her."

"Joseph will chink the house well."

"I'm certain he'll do his best, but a log house is never as warm as a rock one."

"Mr. Hemstead, I know you care about Ruth. But I do, too. I have many things to consider."

"Why not let her stay on at least another year? Or all of you stay on? What could that hurt?" Ruth waited, but no answer came, only silence, until Mr. Hemstead finally spoke again. "What do you say about that, Matthew?"

Again the silence, and then, "Mr. Hemstead, I'm not the one to decide." Ruth heard a certain sad resolve in Matthew's voice. She wished that he would get angry; maybe he could do something. But he said nothing more.

Ruth did feel tired. She had to admit that. In fact, she suddenly felt exhausted. What she wasn't sure about was why she felt that way.

Chapter 13

Joseph knew he had to get out of bed. He couldn't stay down any longer. He sat up, waited for his head to stop swimming, and then he stood up. He had to hold the wall to steady himself. He didn't realize that Brother Engbert had come into the room.

When Joseph had first fallen ill—a few days after the night he had spent in the barn—the Engberts had cleared the little lean-to of a back room for him and made him a bed on the floor. He had been down most of six weeks now. Several times he had resolved to get up and get going, but each time, sometimes only after a few hours, he had lost his will and returned to bed. He had lain there shaking and freezing one minute, burning up the next. Sometimes he wasn't clear about where he was or who was in the room with him.

But during those times when his mind was clear, he was almost in a panic. He had to finish the house he had promised. He had finished cutting trees and brush, and he had prepared a sizable number of logs. He had been almost ready to start raising the house when the illness hit him. He knew the house could be up in a few days, if he got some help. And it could be chinked and ready in two or three weeks. At least, if he had his full strength he could work that fast. Right now, though, he wasn't sure he had the strength to put on his clothes.

"Joseph, you're not ready to go out. Sit up and take a little breakfast, but don't try to go out. This time a year ago I was

86

just as sick as you, and I tried the same thing, thought I had to get back to work. I worked two days and was down two weeks again."

"I'm doing much better," Joseph said, and he swallowed, forcing down the nausea that never seemed to leave him.

"Joseph, some die when they think they're getting better. If you force this thing, you can weaken yourself to the point that you never get well."

But Brother Engbert didn't understand, not fully. He didn't know how much Joseph wanted to marry his daughter. As Joseph lay in bed, all he could think about was that he was doing nothing to earn a living. He had to get a house built for the family and pay what he had promised. Then he had to somehow put together enough money to make at least a down payment on some land of his own. And he had to do it all before this man across the room forced Mary Ann to marry someone else. Brother Engbert didn't know it, but he was Joseph's enemy, and now he was telling him to stay in bed another day.

"I'll walk down to the wood yard and let Brother Andrus know that I'll soon be back. Then I have to have a look at my lot. Maybe I can set the first logs for the house."

"You can't do it, Joseph."

"I'll do it. I'll be all right. It's staying in bed that is eating up my strength."

"That's what I said last year. But it was staying down a little longer that finally got me back to where I could work again."

Joseph paid no attention. He pulled on his shirt and buttoned it. By the time he had gotten on his pantaloons and boots, he was exhausted, but he headed out the door. He knew he should eat, but he couldn't do it. He had vomited until the muscles in his neck and jaw ached. Food was not the answer at the moment.

Joseph made it to the wood yard, or very near it, but he had to stop and lean against a tree. It was there that Brother Andrus came upon him. "Joseph. My goodness, son, you look like a ghost of yourself. Are you sure you should be up and about?"

"Yes. I'm feeling quite well, actually; I'm just a little weak yet. I wanted you to know that I'll be back soon."

"Son, you won't be putting in days chopping wood for quite some time. Certainly not this fall. And the wood business dies out altogether once the river freezes."

Joseph knew all this. He had thought about little else for the last several days. But he had to find some way to earn some money. "Is there maybe . . . some other work?"

"Not that you can do now. Joseph, you'll have to get your strength back through the winter and then come see me next spring. Once you can travel, you better head back to Quincy and winter there with your family."

"I can't do that, Brother Andrus. I promised my family I would get a house ready for them to move into. And I need money for . . . the future."

"If you try to work now, Joseph, you won't have a future. There's some out in the graveyard who learnt that lesson a little too late."

Joseph stood and looked out toward the river. He hated the sickness, but more than that he hated the helplessness. "Do you know of something I can do—while I'm building up my strength?"

"No, I don't. The captain of the boat that put in at the landing a couple of hours ago came looking for a fireman. I told him you were one man I knew who had done some of that work, but I told him you were sick in bed, too. I'm sorry you missed that chance. You could have made a trip or two with him this fall and then wintered in New Orleans. He says there's plenty of work down there."

Maybe this was the answer. Joseph had been praying for some way out of his problem. Maybe this was it. "Did he find someone?"

"I don't know. He's stopping overnight. He said he had to get rid of the drunk he had for a fireman and would have to have a new man by nine o'clock in the morning."

"Thank you, Brother Andrus."

"Joseph, don't try it. The heat from that boiler fire would

sap everything out of you. You'd be dead before a week went by, I promise you."

Joseph was already heading for the landing. And at the dock he mustered up his strength, strode onto the boat, and asked for the captain. In another ten minutes, he was walking back up Joseph Street. He had himself a job. His joy gave him strength for a few minutes, but by the time he reached the Engberts his knees were giving way.

He found Mary Ann in the kitchen with her mother. "Could you step outside just a moment?" he said.

"Joseph," Sister Engbert said, "you're white as a sheet. You better get back to bed right now."

"I need to talk to Mary Ann for a moment, ma'am." He was not usually this forward. The Engberts must have known that he was interested in Mary Ann, but he had never been open about his intentions.

Mary Ann's face colored, but she walked outside with Joseph. He took a breath and tried to call back what strength he could. "I'm leaving, Mary Ann. I just took a job on the *Laura Mae,* a boat at the landing." He saw the startled look on her face. "Don't worry. I'm doing this for us."

"Joseph, you can't go now. You'll kill yourself."

"No. I've got more strength than you think. I have to work this winter. I can't let the time go to waste, and there's no work around here. I'll have to write my family and tell them to delay until next year. Matthew will like that, anyway. I can get some money ahead so I can help pay off the lot, and then I can start saving to put some money on some land for us."

Joseph had never said such a thing to Mary Ann. After the night in the barn, he had let her do most of the talking and hinting, but he had been embarrassed to say much himself. Joseph glanced up now to see if Sister Engbert was close enough to hear. He knew that she and her husband were still hoping Mary Ann would accept an offer from Brother Hall.

"Joseph, you can't do this. If you don't take care of yourself now—if you go to work on that boat—I'll never see you again."

"Oh, yes. You'll see me. I'll be back in the spring, the first

time the river opens up. And I'll have some money in my pocket.
I can't stand to sit here all winter and watch my chances dis-
appear. Your parents aren't going to let up. They won't let you
wait much longer."

"Do you love me that much, Joseph?" She smiled, and her
dimples appeared.

"Yes." Joseph nodded resolutely, as though he had just
struck a bargain with a business partner rather than proclaimed
his love.

"Then stay here. I'll resist my parents. I'll wait until you
can find a way to get us a place. But I won't be responsible for
your running off and killing yourself."

"No, Mary Ann. I've made up my mind. I might not get
another chance like this. I think it's the answer I've been looking
for."

"All summer long you've been telling me that you had to
get that house built by fall, that you had to get your family up
here and Ruth away from the gentiles. How can you change
your mind about all that so suddenly?"

"I haven't changed my mind. I just know that it won't work
to bring them up as the winter sets in. Matthew probably
wouldn't find any work either. That's something I hadn't known
before. It's best to wait until spring now."

"Joseph, take a little more time to think about this. You
jump too fast sometimes. If it's the right thing to do, you can
catch another boat in a couple of weeks when your health isn't
so delicate."

"Not many captains get this far north looking for a fireman,
Mary Ann. I've got my chance now and I have to take it."

Mary Ann stood looking at him for quite some time. "Joseph, please don't do it," she finally said. "Not for me. I think
you'll die, and it will be my fault. I don't want to lose you."

"Just wait for me. I promise to come back in the spring.
Don't marry Brother Hall while I'm gone. That's all I ask."

"Joseph, I promise nothing. I'm against this. I think it's a
terrible mistake. I vow I'll marry him as soon as you walk down
that street."

Joseph wavered at that point, partly because his strength was draining and partly because he wanted her promise before he left. But he wasn't about to let her force him out of this. He had made up his mind.

Joseph walked past Mary Ann and went inside. He passed Sister Engbert, and he knew now that she had been standing close enough to listen. He said nothing, however, just went to his bed, rolled up the blankets, and threw what extra clothes he had in the roll. He grabbed his Book of Mormon and the few personal things he owned and shoved them into an old saddlebag.

As he came back to the door, he met Mary Ann and her mother who were both standing like a blockade. "Joseph," Sister Engbert said, "I'm not opposed to you and Mary Ann, if that's what you both want. But you aren't ready to leave yet. You're putting yourself in great danger."

"I have to do what I think is best, Sister Engbert. If you could look after Mr. Hemstead's horse, I would surely appreciate it."

Mary Ann spoke with fire. "If we take care of it the way you take care of yourself, we'll shoot it tomorrow morning."

"I'd rather you didn't," Joseph said, and he stepped forward and edged between Mary Ann and her mother.

He walked out the door and toward the gate. He didn't like this. He didn't like leaving without more of an agreement. But he wasn't going to lie down and be babied, either. He wasn't going to sit about all winter wishing there were some answer to his dilemma. His way of dealing with things was to take action, get after the problem. Mary Ann had to know that.

As he reached the gate, Mary Ann suddenly ran after him. He saw her coming and he waited. "Joseph, I'll wait for you," she said. "But don't die. Don't let yourself die." She was crying, something Joseph had never seen her do.

"Don't worry. I won't."

"I do worry. So many have died. We haven't told you how many, because we haven't wanted to worry you while you've been down. But Joseph, people are dying every day."

"I'll be fine. I'm feeling a lot better already. And I'll be back next spring. Maybe next summer we can get married. If I stay, I don't know when we could manage it."

Suddenly she had her arms around him. Joseph was very aware that Sister Engbert was watching. He hardly dared to do much more than to pat her gently on the back. "Promise me," she kept saying. "Promise me you won't let yourself die."

"I do promise. And you promise not to marry anyone else."

"I promise," she said, stepping back, but then she came forward again and kissed him. Joseph clung to her just a moment and then moved away. "Oh, Joseph, I've kissed you three times now, and you've never kissed me once."

"I'll kiss you in the spring. I promise." He looked steadily into Mary Ann's eyes. He glanced at Sister Engbert and felt his face grow hot—and not from the fever.

Joseph left. Mary Ann and Sister Engbert wished him God's blessing as he walked away. He took the long walk down Joseph Street feeling stronger than he had in weeks. And when he got on the boat, he sat down to a pretty good meal. He knew he would need his strength. He went to his cabin after that and wrote a letter to his family. He paid a cabin boy to post it.

An hour later he was vomiting up all he had eaten. And he spent the rest of the day and night shaking with cold and then sweating with fever. He wondered at times whether morning would ever come. "Lord, I will not die," he said at one point. He didn't dare state the words as a request; he didn't want to be turned down.

Chapter 14

Home from school, Ruth walked into the kitchen. She let her breath out, felt herself sag a little, and then said, "Hello, Mother."

"Hello, Ruth. How're you feeling today?"

"Fine." She tried to say it with some conviction.

"You don't look fine. I don't see any light in your eyes these days."

"I've just been a little tired, that's all."

"We got a letter from Joseph today."

"How is he doing?"

"Not very well, I'm afraid. He's been sick. He said it hadn't amounted to much, but I don't believe it. He's not been able to work on the house for weeks."

Ruth felt sick herself. Would this mean that Matthew would move them up there and make them live in a wagon or tent while he built the house?

"He's taken a job on a riverboat; he plans to spend the winter in New Orleans. He says he can't get work in Nauvoo. He wants us to stay on here at least until spring."

"Is that what we plan to do?"

Mother looked at Ruth carefully. "Well, there's that light I've been looking for. Your health just came back—in an instant."

"Mother, I didn't—"

"It's all right. It's just as well. Matthew is glad to stay, and the Hemsteads are overjoyed. I don't have to ask how you feel about it."

But Mother seemed disappointed. Ruth didn't know what to say to her.

"Get your homework done, if you have any. I'll need help with supper before long."

"Yes, ma'am." Ruth slipped out of the kitchen quickly, trying not to walk with too much spring in her step. But when she got upstairs, she could hardly contain her joy. She did her homework and then went downstairs to help her mother. She tried not to look too happy. But when Mr. Hemstead came in, the first thing he said was, "My, my, is this the same little girl? She looks better than I've seen her in weeks. I think she could slip that blue satin dress on and go off dancing this very night."

"Yes," Mother said, "I think that's exactly what she would like to do."

Ruth caught the glance, heard the sarcasm. And it stung. Why did Mother always think the worst of her? She didn't want to move to Nauvoo, but that hardly seemed the sin that Mother made it into. In fact, somewhere in the jumble of her emotions was a hint of disappointment—if only for one reason. She did miss Joseph terribly, and she had looked forward to seeing him. She hoped he was all right.

Joseph was little more than a skeleton by the time he reached New Orleans. He was barely able to hold down enough food and water to survive, and the boiler fire made him sweat until he lost much of the liquid he could keep in his stomach. The captain was not a bad man; he could have been much worse. But he needed a fireman and thought he had hired one. He offered Joseph a chance to leave the boat at St. Louis, but he offered no free rides to New Orleans where work was supposed to be available in the winter.

Joseph stayed on. He hauled wood and stoked the fire. At times he lay on the deck for half an hour thinking that he would never get up; but then he always thought of Mary Ann, and he prodded himself back up with his constant vow: "I won't die. I promised." Sometimes, however, he wished that he could. The chance to rest seemed so inviting.

When he finally reached New Orleans, he rented a depressing little room in an old boarding house and went to bed. It was two and half weeks before he stepped outside again, and by then most of the money he had made on board the *Laura Mae* was gone. Room and board were expensive, and now he was hearing that while there were some jobs about, far too much labor was available.

Joseph was holding food down now, and he was gradually feeling his strength return, but he looked like a specter, which hardly served as a recommendation for a job at hard labor. For a solid week he went about town asking after work. Most people were fairly polite but simply said they had nothing. Others told him he needed to put on a little flesh before he thought about looking for work.

Joseph was getting desperate. If he didn't find work he would not have the money to pay for his board and room, let alone save anything toward the land he hoped to buy. He couldn't stand the thought of going back to Mary Ann with less hope for the future than when he had left Nauvoo.

He eventually checked back with a warehouse on the docks where a man had told him there might be some work in time. At first the man said that nothing had opened up, but then, just as Joseph was about to walk away, he asked, "You speak very well. I take it you can read and write."

"Yes, sir."

"How do you do with numbers? Have you ever done any bookkeeping?"

"No, sir. But it's something I can learn. I did very well with arithmetic in school."

The man nodded. Joseph started to pray.

"I need a man who can read orders and pass them along to the dock workers, someone who can keep books, and someone who could write out a letter for me from time to time."

"I could do all that, sir."

"Well, I was hoping for someone with experience, but such a man hasn't shown himself. I guess I could give you a try. But are you well? Your color isn't good at all."

"I've been sick, sir, but I'm coming back now. In two weeks you won't know me. I'm not usually so thin."

"Well, all right. But just as a try. In one week, if you can't do what I need, I'll have to let you go. Be here by seven o'clock in the morning, and I'll get you started. The pay is better than dock work—it's a dollar and a half a day—but I have to have a man who can take some responsibility. I wouldn't usually hire a young fellow like yourself."

"You'll find me responsible, sir. You won't be sorry."

"I think that might be right. You're not the usual breed we get around these docks."

Joseph went back to his room and prayed to thank the Lord for his good fortune. He had felt right about this trip to New Orleans, and now he seemed justified. A dollar and a half a day was twice what he expected to make. The money would stack up fast now, and he could make up for the lost time.

Mary Ann was sitting by the fire. It was Christmas Day. The early darkness was already setting in. Her little brother and sister were excited. Amy had a new doll with a real china face, and Robert a stick horse. Malinda had received a lovely new dress, and so had Mary Ann. The dresses were not fancy, but they were made from store-bought calico, not homespun. Mary Ann had not expected so much.

Father was sitting next to her and peeling an apple with his penknife. The children liked apples on Christmas, baked with brown sugar in the coals of the fire. But Father liked a fresh apple better than anything.

"Is Brother Hall going to call on you this evening?" Brother Engbert asked.

"I believe so. He said he would."

"Don't sound so happy."

Mary Ann glanced at her father, sure she knew what was

coming next. "Father, let's not start this again. I have never encouraged him to call. I have never let him think that I am interested in him. You have done more to give him hope than I have."

"Mary Ann, I ought to do what's best for you. I ought to command you to take this man for a husband. He's a fine person, better educated than most, and true to the gospel. There's not one reason in the world for you to turn him down."

"Would it make any difference if I said that I didn't love him?"

"That's girl talk, Mary Ann. And you're nearly grown into a woman. You need to consider more than just the way a man looks, or whether he pleases with every word he says. I wish your older sister could have started out as well as you would with him."

"Father, Brother Hall looks well enough, and he talks fine. I just happen not to find him someone I want to marry. Did someone force you to marry Mother, or did you choose her for yourself?"

Brother Engbert smiled just a little. "I chose her, but I'm not so sure she would have chosen me if other choices had been available."

Sister Engbert was getting the apples ready for baking. She laughed from across the room. "It was him or nothing," she said. "And I said, 'Nothing is too good for me.' "

"Do you see where you get that spiked tongue of yours, Mary Ann?"

Mary Ann laughed, and hoped that the subject was changed now. She did want to laugh and talk, and not argue with her father. She was having a hard enough time not giving way to sadness this day. She had gotten one letter from Joseph, shortly after he had arrived in New Orleans. He had said he was doing much better, but his writing was shaky and weak, no matter what the words said. Since then, nothing had come; and now that the river was frozen, mail would come rarely, if at all. For all she knew, Joseph was dead. He could promise all he wanted, but lots of others in Nauvoo had gone to a reward they would rather have waited for. The Prophet's father had died just a few days after Joseph had left for New Orleans, and he was only one of hundreds.

"Mary Ann, I want you to be happy in your marriage. I want you to choose a man you fancy. But it's easy enough to trick yourself in these matters. I fear that you set your heart on Joseph Williams back there in Far West, and now you won't let go. You're so stubborn that you cling to a notion once it gets in your head—whether it's best for you or not."

Father had actually never admitted before that he knew Mary Ann's preference. For some reason, the mention of Joseph embarrassed Mary Ann. But she didn't let it stop her tongue. "Maybe I should tell you that once you set your mind on Mother, you should have changed it once in a while, just to show that you weren't stubborn."

Mother laughed again. "Answer that one if you can," she said.

"Now, that's quite another thing. Once you give your promise and commitment to a man, there's no stepping back from that. But you don't have to assume that some girlish notion you have about a boy—a boy not even fully grown—is a lifetime promise."

"You said I'm grown now."

"Nearly."

"Well, close enough that you want me to set up housekeeping with Brother Hall. I guess that's grown."

"No, no. I'm in no rush for you to marry. There's time for that. But Brother Hall is a grown man, and he'll want to know what your intentions are."

"He *would* know if he had enough brains to see what he was seeing."

Father laughed again. "Well, Mary Ann, you're too much for me. I never could talk you in or out of anything. And I will say that I like Joseph Williams just fine. But he's hardly more than a boy, has not a prospect in the world for anything but breaking his back on some rocky farm here about, and as far as I'm concerned he's not one lick easier to love than Brother

Hall. I can't see why you can't love a man with a little more to offer."

Mary Ann had lots of quick answers. She could tell Father that he was a farmer himself, and by his own standards no catch. She could tell him that Brother Hall had an irritating way of looking at her, as though he were studying a newspaper, full of concentration but no enthusiasm. She could tell him that Joseph was not just a handsome boy; he was a young man who dreamed, a young man who would do something with his life.

But what she chose to say probably pleased her father best. "When Joseph Williams was a little boy, I think nine or ten, the Prophet told him he had an important mission in this life. He said that if he stayed true to the Church he would play a great role in building the kingdom. He is true to the Church, Father. You'll see what he'll be someday, and you'll congratulate me for my choice."

Her father gave Mary Ann a long, serious look, and then he nodded. "I guess you've thought more about this than I give you credit for."

"I guess I have," Mary Ann said, and she was very pleased. But then she laughed. "Of course, the young fool will probably never live through the winter."

"He'll live," Mother said. "Come spring, he'll show up. If the river doesn't open up, he'll throw a riverboat up on his back and walk on the ice all the way here. I saw the look in his eye when he promised you."

Chapter 15

The winter passed away quietly for Mary Ann, who counted the days until spring. She eventually got a letter from Joseph that told of his good fortune in finding work and of his returning health. Mary Ann read the letter every day and she watched the weather, wondering when the riverboats would first begin to ply the Mississippi.

Joseph's winter passed just as slowly, but every time he added a week's pay to what he already had, he told himself that he was closer to his goal. He was better off than he might have been, sitting out the winter in Nauvoo. All the same, he had never been so lonely in his life. The dreary room he lived in gradually came to symbolize a jail cell, nearly as ugly and cramped as the jail in Liberty, where he had seen the Prophet.

But like the Prophet, Joseph turned the time into something worthwhile. He studied the Book of Mormon as he never had before. No longer was he doing it to satisfy someone else's idea about what he ought to be doing; he was finally looking to deepen his understanding. He found his heroes in Nephi and in Alma the Younger—young men new to their callings but ready to serve. Joseph wanted the same power of spirit, the same dedication. As his physical strength returned, his spirit seemed to fill out the new layers of flesh. He knew his time away from Nauvoo, from Mary Ann, had been well spent.

The weather in New Orleans was deceiving. He found it hard to believe that the upper Mississippi could be gripped with winter when the temperatures were so mild where he was. He listened for news of conditions to the north and hoped for an early spring.

It was late March when Joseph took passage upriver. He had forced himself to stay on longer than he really wanted to, but it meant a little more money to take back. He decided not to hire on as a fireman; no one would want a one-way man on the crew. So he paid his way, although only as a deck passenger. Expenses had eaten up a good share of what he had earned, but he was pleased that he had saved eighty-four dollars during the winter. Some of it would go toward paying off the family land—along with whatever Matthew and Mother could pay. But he thought he probably had a healthy start on a payment for some land of his own.

On deck the first day he met a pair of young men, brothers, not much older than himself. They were heading for St. Louis, they said, and after that, west into Oregon country. "We'll make a go of it, one way or another," the older brother said. He grinned, and then he spit over the rail into the river, not seeming to worry that some of the tobacco juice had dribbled onto his thick beard. He was a big fellow, and he spoke with a strong accent. He sounded like the men from Virginia and Kentucky that Joseph had known in Missouri.

"We might try some trappin'," the other brother said. He laughed for some reason; both of them did. The younger brother was not quite as tall, but he was every bit as stout. Between the two of them, they looked ready to take on about anything.

"Lots of trappers used to come and go from Independence," Joseph said. "I lived near there at one time. I think some of them did pretty well, but all the outfitting doesn't come cheap."

"I guess that's right," the older one said, and then he asked what Joseph had been doing way out in western Missouri. Joseph hesitated, never sure what to expect when he told someone he was a Mormon. He had taken some abuse from a couple of men in the boarding house in New Orleans. But the brothers seemed quite interested. They said they had heard of Mormons, but they didn't know much about them. "But my brother and me,

we're both the church-going kind; at least we were brought up
that way."

For the first time in Joseph's life, he really felt ready to be
a missionary. He saw the chance to be like Alma, to sit down
with these two young men—simple, but good men—and preach
to them with the power of his own conviction. Maybe before he
was finished they would come on to Nauvoo instead of heading
west. Maybe they would do as Alma's converts had done and
continue to spread the gospel.

Joseph stayed close to the men and learned their names—
Jed and Alex Stott. As often as he could, he led the conversation
around to the gospel. Eventually, he took out his Book of Mormon, read them passages, and explained the doctrines. He told
them about Joseph Smith—how he had received the ancient
records and translated them. He told them about his own ac-
quaintance with the man and bore testimony of his power as a
prophet.

Jed and Alex listened, asked questions, and took the dis-
cussion very seriously. Joseph didn't know whether they were
moving toward conversion, but at least he felt secure in his
ability to teach and explain. He would be a good missionary; he
felt sure of that now.

On the third night out of New Orleans, not long after Joseph
had rolled out his blankets and made his bed on deck, the
brothers came to him. "Joseph," Jed whispered, "could we
speak to you for a minute?"

Joseph heard the concern in his voice. He hoped they were
wrestling with the gospel and needed some further answers. He
got up. He followed the men to the stern of the boat.

"Listen, Joseph," Jed said, "we're a might worried for you.
We jiss heard some talk that don't sound good."

"What do you mean? What kind of talk?"

"Remember you told us you went south for the winter to
earn some money and save it up?"

"Yes."

"There must be some folks who heard what you said. We
heard a couple of fellers talking, and the one said to the other,

'If that boy's got his winter's earnings with him, we might just have that and throw him in the river.' "

A chill passed through Joseph. He glanced over to see whether anyone was near enough to hear, but most of the deck passengers stayed well forward, away from the noise of the big stern wheel.

"Are you carrying the money with you, Joseph?"

"Yes, I am."

"Have you put it in a safe place?"

"Well, I had thought so. I sewed it into the lining of this coat."

"Joseph, that wasn't wise. Most folks will look for it there right off."

"What should I do with it?"

Jed was still doing all the talking. "They have a safe on board. You can put it there. No deck passenger ever ought to carry his own money. There's bad folks that travel these boats; they don't care one bit that yer a religious feller."

"Thanks for letting me know, Jed. I'm thinking maybe I can go up and talk to the pilot right now. Maybe he has a place for the money for the night, and then I can get it into a safe in the morning."

"Yes, that's a good thought. But one thing. If some men did throw you over, could you make a good swim of it? Could you make it to shore?"

Joseph looked out into the darkness. There was a little moonlight, and Joseph thought the shore was less than a quarter of a mile. "I probably could, if I could get my coat and boots off. But I wouldn't want to try. I hope you two fellows will stay close to me tonight."

"Don't worry about that." Joseph hadn't noticed that Alex had worked his way behind him.

When he saw Jed nod to him, he suddenly had a terrible thought, but by then he already felt Alex's big hand clamp over his mouth. "Don't worry at all," Alex said, "we'll take off your coat and boots. We wouldn't want you to drown." He had pulled

Joseph close to his chest. His laugh was wet and gurgly in Joseph's ear.

For just a moment Joseph put up a struggle, but Alex tightened his grip, pressuring Joseph's jaw with one hand and his chest with the other. The man could break his neck in an instant, and he knew it.

Jed pulled off Joseph's coat, reaching around and pulling it down over Joseph's still rather thin shoulders and off his back. "Make sure the money's there," Alex said. "He might be lying."

"He don't have enough brains to lie," Jed said, laughing. "The money's here. I can feel it." He reached down then and grabbed Joseph's feet, one at a time, and jerked off his boots. "I don't guess these'll fit me or you, Alex. Maybe we can sell 'em to some of these bad folks on deck."

"All right now, Joseph," Alex said, close to his ear. "We'll throw you well clear of this here paddle, and you start swimming when you hit the water. And pray plenty. That's what me and Jed's gonna do from now on when we git in a fix. You done a good job o' teaching us all about that."

Jed grabbed Joseph's feet, and the two men swung Joseph out and over the rail. Joseph let out one shout, more from fear than any hope of getting help, but once he hit the water, he followed Alex's advice. He began to swim immediately. He knew he had his work cut out for him. The water was still very high, the river wide, and the current strong. He would have to go with the current but fight his way over toward the shore.

"Help me, Lord," he said. "Help me, Lord." He drove his arms forward in the water and kicked with all his might. "Please, Lord. Don't let me die now."

The help came. His shoulder bumped up against some driftwood—a log—and he grabbed on tight. He saved his strength for a time and then began to kick to try and work himself closer to shore. At the first bend in the river, a sand bar jutted out, and Joseph suddenly felt his feet hit bottom. He let go of the log and tumbled over once as he was pushed by the current. But soon he worked his way into more shallow water and onto the bank itself.

He dropped onto the grass and tried to get his breath. He was thankful he had made it, thankful to be alive. For some time that was his only thought. He muttered his thanks to the Lord.

But he had not even stopped praying when he thought of Jed and Alex telling him to do just that. Suddenly his own stupidity overwhelmed him. Why had he even bothered to make a swim for it? How would he get to Nauvoo now? How could he face Mary Ann when he got there? Every cent he had in the world was gone. His whole winter's work was lost. Everything he thought he had gained was wiped out—by the very men he thought he was converting.

He lay on the grass and looked toward the heavens. "Why?" he said. He slammed his fists into the sand, felt that old anger he had known so many times already in his life. Why was there never any fairness in this world? He slammed down his fist again and again, holding back the tears that way.

Ruth was standing at the window of her room, looking out across the fields through a driving blizzard. The spring storm had begun the night before and had continued all day. Missing school was not a joy to her. She knew that the days with Emmie and Miss Gordon would not last much longer, anyway. The delay in moving on to Nauvoo had made her happy, but the winter had passed away all the same, and now Matthew and Mother were making plans to move on once the spring planting was completed. Ruth could wish for a cold spring, but the best that would do was delay the move a week or two.

"It's not letting up at all, is it?" It was Mr. Hemstead. He often came up to look out this window on such a day, because the view was best from there.

"Not at all."

"Ruth, are you well these days? You've looked rather tired again lately."

Ruth knew that this was as much a hope as anything. He still wanted her to stay. "No, I'm fine."

"You have grown this winter. I've noticed how tall you're getting."

"I guess I've outgrown the pretty dress you gave me."

He didn't speak. Ruth knew he was as sad as she was that she hadn't worn it—except for the time that had gotten her into trouble.

"Mr. Hemstead?"

"Yes?"

"Was it lovely in the East—in Boston?"

"Well, I suppose. I like it here better, all things considered, but I know my wife doesn't feel the same way."

"Did you take her to fancy parties?"

"Yes. And Martha loved that. I didn't mind it so much, either—but I'm not much for dancing. I just loved the sight of her in those beautiful gowns, with her hair all done up so pretty. She was a beautiful woman then."

"She's pretty now."

"Yes, she is. I think so. I'm glad you think so, too, Ruth. Not every young person would see what's so pretty behind the wrinkles and the gray hair."

"It's her eyes, and her smile."

"Exactly. It's what you have, too, Ruth. And you've got that pretty hair—much like Martha used to have. And little Mary. She had such beautiful hair."

"You still miss her, don't you?"

"Of course. I always will. But I hope you know that I no longer think of you as her replacement. I've come to like you for yourself."

Ruth did know that.

"My offer still holds."

"Mother won't let me stay, Mr. Hemstead. And anyway, it's not a farm I want." She looked at him and smiled. "I want to live in Boston."

"Maybe I shouldn't say this," Mr. Hemstead said, "but if that's what I wanted, I would find a way. That's how I do things. I go after the things I want."

"I guess I do, too," Ruth said. But it was something she

wanted to believe more than something she was sure of, just yet.

"You've been brought up a certain way—among good people. But Mormons have a way of doing things that is different from most, and there comes a time when a young person has to make a choice. Not all decide to do exactly as their parents have done. But I don't mean to—"

"It's all right. I know I have to make my choice."

"I'll just say one more thing, Ruth. People around here felt sorry for the Mormons when they first came. But the mood is changing. Your Joseph Smith has a lot of power in Hancock County now—some say too much. I don't know what will come of it all, but I don't like what I'm hearing people say."

"Will they try to hurt us again? Will they burn our houses down?"

"I don't know, Ruth. I wouldn't think so. But I do think you would all be better off not to gather up in one place. I still don't see why you have to do that."

Ruth watched the snow. The big flakes were being driven by a hard, steady wind. The rush of flakes, angling past the window, was like the flow of a great waterfall. The power of it was frightening. Ruth wondered whether a single flake had the power to resist the force, to go its own way. But she couldn't see any that did.

Chapter 16

Joseph stood before the Engberts' door for some time. He wanted to see Mary Ann more than anything in the world, but for three weeks he had been dreading the thought of telling her how stupid he had been. He had spent a week walking and most of the rest working in a wood yard, chopping enough wood to pay passage on another riverboat—and to buy a new pair of boots.

He finally knocked, and when Mary Ann opened the door herself, and shouted for joy, he momentarily forgot about his disappointment. She jumped forward and caught him around the neck, "Oh, Joseph, kiss me this time. Kiss me before I kiss you."

Joseph did, but she jumped back almost immediately. "What's the matter?" she said. "Is something wrong?"

"Well, I . . . I had some bad luck on the way back."

She looked concerned. "What kind of bad luck?"

"I guess it wasn't bad luck at all." He looked down, wishing he didn't have to say it. "It was plain stupidity. I let some men steal everything I earned all winter. I don't have a dime of it."

"Oh, Joseph."

He saw her disappointment, and something inside him sank. He had let her down entirely.

"Come inside. Tell me what happened. Tell me everything."

Joseph did go inside, said hello to Sister Engbert and the younger children, and then he told his story. He told it all, and he went out of his way to make himself look as foolish as possible. "I'll never forgive myself," he finally said. "I've nothing now, and I promised you everything."

"You promised me that you would come back—alive—and you did."

He wanted to say more, to express his disappointment that he had nothing with which to buy land to begin something for them, but he was too self-conscious to say that in front of Sister Engbert.

"Joseph, you trusted those men. That was your only mistake. You tried to teach them to be Christians, and you treated them in a Christian way. That's not so bad a fault. It was your goodness that made you think well of them."

Sister Engbert said, "If it's a fault, it's one you share with Brother Joseph. He's trusted people who have done him great harm—and he's done it more than once."

"Once is enough for me," Joseph said.

"Don't say that, Joseph. Don't be bitter. I'd rather see you lose all the money you ever earn than become bitter and angry."

Joseph knew what Mary Ann was saying, but the idea bothered him. He almost wished she would show more disappointment, let him know that she hated the idea of a delay in their marriage.

"Is Mr. Hemstead's horse still with you?" Joseph said. He wanted to change the subject.

"Yes."

"I'll pay your father—when I can—for the feed. Right now I need to take the horse and ride to Quincy. I need to talk to Mother and Matthew. I don't know how to tell them all this in a letter. We need to talk things out. I just walked by our lot; every log I cut last summer is gone. I have to start all over on that, too."

"Joseph, people who got here in the winter were desperate. They had to get their families inside. If you ask around, people will tell you who took the logs. They'll cut more for you. I'm sure they will."

"Yes, I'll probably get my boots back, too. Those nice fellows just borrowed them." Joseph smiled, joylessly. He thought of the week he had spent walking over rocky roads, his stockings worn through and his feet bleeding.

"Joseph, please don't. I wanted you back more than just alive. I wanted the same Joseph back. Don't change," Mary Ann pleaded.

Joseph nodded and said nothing for a time, but then he said, "In any case, I think I'll head out today so that I can talk things over with my family. I'll be back in a few days. I do feel strong now. At least I'm ready to work."

"That's good. Things will be fine." Mary Ann took Joseph by the hand and gave it a squeeze.

Joseph looked up at Sister Engbert. She seemed to know that he was embarrassed. She smiled, and then she walked into the other room of their cabin. Joseph took the chance to say, "Mary Ann, I had eighty-four dollars. By the end of the summer I could have maybe bought us a piece of land. We could have gotten married."

"Married? Is that what you want? You want to marry me, Joseph?"

"Mary Ann, don't, all right?"

"But Joseph, you never asked me to marry you."

"Yes, I did. In a way. You know that's what I want."

"So then, ask me."

"I have to talk to your father first." He couldn't help smiling a little.

"You know better than that. He tells me himself that he can't talk me out of anything."

"He would talk you out of me if he could, wouldn't he?"

"No. I don't think so. But don't change the subject. Ask me."

"Not now, Mary Ann. It's not the right time. I need to get something going again. I need to have something to offer you."

"Joseph, Brother Hall has been coming around all winter. If you're not interested in me, tell me now, because I do have other prospects."

"Come on, Mary Ann. Don't make me—"

"Ask me, Joseph."

Joseph looked in those pretty eyes, and he felt himself sink all the way in. "Will you marry me, Mary Ann?"

"Yes."

But why that devilish smile of hers? he wondered suddenly. "I don't know whether you're joking or not, Mary Ann. Why do you have to smile like that?"

"Because I'm happy."

"I am too."

"I know you are. That's why I'm happy. I can see the old you coming back."

"Aren't you happy I asked you to marry me?"

"Not much. I knew we'd get married. I just wanted to make you smile."

Joseph shook his head. It would be no easy time keeping up with her all his life.

"Joseph, don't you know what you should do now?"

"No. What?"

"You should kiss me. You just asked me to marry you, and I just said yes. You've got to learn when you're supposed to kiss me. I can't be doing this for you all our lives."

Joseph glanced toward the other room.

"It's okay. She won't be shocked. After all, we're engaged."

So Joseph kissed her, but only rather quickly. It's not that he didn't like the kissing; he was just worried to death that Sister Engbert would step through the door—or that one of the children would.

"Joseph, you have a lot to learn about kissing."

Joseph took a long look at her. "What are you telling me? That the other men who kiss you do it better?"

"Not at all. You're the only man—or boy—I've ever kissed. But I still think it's supposed to be better than that. You kiss like you're afraid of touching."

Truth be known, Joseph *was* a little afraid of touching—at least for the moment. Somehow he had to start all over, and so he couldn't indulge himself too much yet. "I guess I'll get better in time," he said. "You can teach me — since you think you know so much about it."

But he didn't do any more practicing then. He got up and went outside to saddle his horse. Mary Ann told him about the things that had been happening in Nauvoo. The cornerstone for the temple had been laid just a week before. And plans were being made for a beautiful hotel. The apostles in England were reporting wonderful success, and thousands of people were entering the Church — many of them planning to immigrate to Nauvoo.

"We're going to prosper here, Joseph. It's all beginning to happen. I think there will be more work this summer — more building — with so many moving in. And if you talk to Brother Joseph and tell him that we want to get married, I know he'll help you get some land someway. We'll work things out."

Joseph was almost afraid to think so. For three weeks he had avoided all optimism, afraid that his disappointment would be complete when he reached Nauvoo. He told himself a thousand times that Mary Ann would give him up and take a better man. But she still had faith in him. In spite of himself, he began to feel that things were not so bad.

When Joseph arrived at the Hemstead farm, he spotted Matthew in the field, those familiar, powerful legs silhouetted against the sunset, driving forward behind his team, getting in a last half hour of work. Joseph had feared telling Mary Ann what had happened to him, but he had known he would have to do it. In Matthew's case, Joseph felt something deeper than fear. Joseph's story would make him look like a little boy. That's what he had told himself he was as he lay there on that riverbank in the dark, but he didn't want Matthew to think it.

So Joseph went inside the house, greeted Mother and Ruth and the Hemsteads. Then Matthew came in and grabbed Joseph and hugged him more powerfully than he ever had before. "It's so good to see you," he said. "I'm so proud of you. You did very well for yourself this winter."

"No, Matthew," Joseph said, "I didn't. I have some bad news."

Joseph sat down and told his story again, this time explaining a little more how he had been taken in by the apparent interest the brothers had shown for the gospel.

"But Joseph," Matthew said, "didn't it occur to you that you shouldn't tell them where you had hidden the money?"

Joseph looked at the floor. "No, it didn't. I thought I was Alma, I guess, and I thought they were my brothers in the gospel. I know it sounds stupid, but that's what I thought."

"It doesn't sound stupid at all to me," Mother said.

"All the same," Matthew said, "a man can't be too careful. You should have seen something coming when they asked where your money was."

"I know, Matthew. I know that. Don't think I'm not aware of that . . . now."

"It's just that in the future you'll have to—"

"Matthew, I know. All right?"

"Well, sure. Sometimes we have to learn things the hard way. It's just the thought of losing everything you earned, all winter long—it's hard to imagine that you wouldn't have been a little more careful with that much money."

There was nothing to say to that. In another minute, Matthew excused himself to go back outside to finish his chores. Joseph knew that he should help. Instead, he sat there, staring into the fire in the fireplace.

Mr. Hemstead finally spoke. "Joseph, you've gone out in the world. You made a mistake. Matthew stayed here. He doesn't know what might have happened had he done the same as you. Only a man who pokes his nose out in the wind finds out what it is to get it frozen. But those who never do never smell much of this world."

Joseph nodded, and then he looked about. Mother said that was right, and so did Mrs. Hemstead. But Ruth was looking at him intently, as though she wanted to say something or at least signal that she understood. For some reason that consoled him more than anything.

Chapter 17

The next morning Ruth left early for school, and then she turned up the trail towards Emmie's house and met her halfway to the road. "Good morning," Emmie called out, obviously overjoyed that Ruth had made the extra effort. But almost immediately she seemed to see something in Ruth's face. "What's the matter?"

"Joseph got back last night. He talked with Matthew and Mother. We're leaving for sure. As soon as the crops are planted and Mr. Hemstead can find someone to take over."

"Oh, Ruth. They've said that before, but every time you stay anyway. I don't think Matthew really wants to go."

"I know he doesn't. But this time we're going. Mother says we can't put it off any longer. Joseph's going back to build a house. We'll be gone in no more than two months."

"Oh, Ruth. My heart is breaking."

"Don't, Emmie."

"Don't what?"

"Don't be silly. It isn't funny to me."

"Funny? Is that what you think? You think that I'm laughing?"

"Yes. Or at least you don't try to understand how I feel."

"Ruth, you're my dearest friend, and I'm about to be left in this desolate place without a companion to share my pain and my joys. And I'll tell you what else I'm feeling. It's time to be sick again."

Ruth shook her head. "Oh, Emmie, that won't work. I've been healthy for almost a year. They won't believe I'm having a relapse."

"It could be a whole new sickness. We have a book at home that tells all about diseases. We could look something up and learn every symptom, and you could—"

"Emmie, no. I don't want to do that."

"You're giving up, Ruth. You're giving up all your dreams. The next time I hear of you, you'll be married to a stout little farmer with manure on his boots and the elbows out of his only decent suit coat. 'It's good enough for the likes of me,' he'll tell you. 'I pray every day and thank the Lord that I have a coat this good.' And he'll have that kind of mouth that makes creases straight down at the corners because he thinks it's against his religion to smile."

"Emmie, I'm not going to marry anyone like that. And Mormons aren't so stern as you think." But Ruth decided she wouldn't argue anymore. In fact, she wondered why she had bothered to come and tell Emmie. She was not really a help.

"What about Boston, Ruth? Are you giving up all hope of that? Remember the parties? Remember entering the beautiful ball, in our perfect gowns, and our names being read? Remember walking down the steps and into the grand ballroom and everyone looking at us?"

"Yes, I remember. Better than you."

"What do you mean by that?"

"Emmie, for you it's something to talk and dream about. For me it's something real, and something I want. Twenty years from now, you'll be reading those newspapers and dreaming your dreams when you're married to some boy from around here. But I'll be there. I'm going to find a way."

"Ruth, really?"

"Yes. Really."

"You sound so serious. Your mind is made up, isn't it?"

"Yes, Emmie. It's not just pretend with me the way it is with you."

"Ruth, that is very unkind." She walked on for a time before she added, "I suppose it's true, but very unkind. Are you really going?"

But Ruth had lost interest in talking. In truth, she had lost interest in Emmie. Somehow, in the last year she had outgrown her—even though Emmie was older. Emmie may not have to look at reality for quite some time, but for Ruth reality was something she couldn't avoid. It was a log house in Nauvoo. It was homespun dresses and worn-out boots. It was going back to what she had always known before the dream interrupted her reality. Emmie had always lived in a fine, rock farmhouse, had always worn pretty dresses to church, had never been forced out of her house, had never been hated. She didn't even know what to fear.

The next week passed quickly. The weather was fair, and the planting was moving ahead. Matthew hired a young man to help, the same man who would soon take over the farm. Ruth knew it broke Matthew's heart to give over everything, to release control of this place he loved so much.

At school, Ruth found herself daydreaming much of the time, struggling even to pay attention. One morning she was not listening when Miss Gordon asked her a question.

"Ruth, are you with us today?"

Suddenly Ruth heard her name and realized she had no idea what she had been asked. "Yes, ma'am."

"Then answer the question."

"I'm sorry. What was it?"

"Never mind. I'll ask someone who is still among the living. I don't know what's gotten into you lately, but you haven't been the scholar you are capable of being. I hate to see you waste your ability." Everyone was looking, and Ruth was humiliated. Miss Gordon hadn't any idea what Ruth was going through right now.

Ruth felt sorry for herself all day, and by the time school was out she didn't want to talk to anyone. She hurried out of school and walked fast. She knew that Emmie could never get away quickly, what with all the talking she always did; and once out the door, she wasn't capable of walking very fast. She would be shocked to know that Ruth had left her behind, but she wouldn't catch up.

Ruth walked resolutely, not in a hurry to get home, but just in a hurry to get off by herself. She reached the road and then slowed some, knowing she was beyond the point where Emmie could even see her. But as soon as she started down the road, she noticed someone — a man, it appeared — sitting on the rail fence, maybe half a mile ahead. This made her nervous. She really didn't want to walk past him, but there was no other way to go.

She had come fairly close, only glancing at the person occasionally, when he looked up at her and said hello.

"Justin." She didn't know if she should walk on by. Was he waiting for her?

"Could I talk to you for a minute or two?"

Ruth stopped, and she nodded. She felt very strange. She hadn't seen him all spring. He looked grown-up.

"I'm done with school, Ruth. My father needs me every day now. He would like me to go back another year, but I can see it isn't going to happen. There's too much to keep up all the time. I could come over for a time in the dead of winter, but I doubt there's much point to that."

Ruth had no idea how to respond. Had he come and waited here just to tell her that? Was he saying good-bye?

"I'm just helping my father for now. But he's about to buy some more land — a big piece just down from where we farm now. It's good land. It needs some clearing, but it will make a good farm. He says it will be mine after a time."

Ruth nodded, and finally made herself say, "That's nice, Justin."

He had gotten down from the fence, and now he was standing directly in front of Ruth, holding his hat in his hands. He seemed to have lost his own sense of purpose. Ruth could see he was as embarrassed as she was by the silence.

"I saw Emmie at church on Sunday. She says you'll be moving away soon."

"That's right." She glanced up at him, but he looked away quickly.

"Ruth, I. . . . " He stopped for quite some time, and finally Ruth took another look. Once again, he glanced away, avoiding her eyes. "I wish you weren't leaving."

This was all too much for Ruth. She wanted to run, to not have to stand there; yet, she wanted him to say more, to say what he really had in mind.

"You won't be so far away, upriver fifty miles or so. Maybe I'll ride up there and see you someday—when we're both older."

Ruth couldn't think what to say. Then on impulse, she told him what she had been thinking. "Justin, I don't want to move to Nauvoo. I don't want to live there. I want to live in the East somewhere. Maybe Boston. That's what I hope more than anything." Somehow it mattered to her that he know that; and yet, she could see he didn't know what to make of it.

"I have some hopes, too. I'd like to start out with a big farm and do my best with it. But I'd like to start up some gristmills, or maybe a sawmill. My father and I talk a lot about that. I'm the only son, and I'll get his land in time, too. He says if I do things just right, someday I might own plenty of land around here, and mills, and maybe a bank or something like that. He says there's no reason I couldn't be as rich as Mr. Musgrave in Quincy, the one that owns the bank and the store."

"I hope you can do that, Justin. That would be . . . very nice."

"I guess it'll work out."

"I think it probably will."

Again they had run out of things to say. They looked toward, but not really at, each other.

"Emmie says you don't want to be a Mormon and marry one of those poor farmers who's running off all the time to go out preaching."

Ruth had never said that—not exactly. These were Emmie's words. And yet, Ruth could hardly deny them.

"I don't think you're like most of the Mormons. I think you would—"

"What do you mean by that?"

"You're not all crazy with religion, the way some of those people are."

"Mormons aren't any crazier than anyone else." Ruth was a little surprised at herself. She didn't mean to sound angry, and yet her voice was intense.

"Well, I'm sorry. I didn't mean to insult anyone. I just mean that so many Mormons seem to want to spend their whole lives preaching and praying and acting like that's all there is to life. You're not like that. You're like everyone else."

"Justin, you don't know one thing about Mormons. They aren't at all like that. They farm and build gristmills and open up banks and do everything you talk about doing. My brothers can farm with anyone around here."

"Ruth, I didn't mean to—"

"I don't care what you meant to do. You're like everyone else. You make up your mind about something you don't know anything about."

"Ruth, you're the one who said you didn't want to live in Nauvoo."

"That's true. I don't want to live there."

"Well, do you want to be a Mormon, or don't you?"

Ruth was looking at him now, not so self-conscious, but she had no answer. "That's my own business," she finally said. And she walked away.

"Ruth, I only came over to say good-bye."

Ruth stopped and turned around. "Thank you. Good-bye, Justin. I didn't mean to snap at you. I just don't think you could ever . . . ." She didn't know how to finish the sentence. Every time she thought she knew her own mind, something made her doubt herself all over again. "I'm glad you came to say good-bye."

"Should I come see you in Nauvoo?"

"If you like."

"Would your mother mind?"

"Probably."

He looked her in the eyes longer than he ever had before. "It's kind of a muddle, isn't it?" he said. It was as close as he came to saying what was really on his mind.

Ruth said it was and she walked on, but she hadn't gone twenty feet before tears were in her eyes. Justin had no idea how great the muddle was.

Chapter 18

Ruth sat next to Matthew up front in the wagon. She had always called Nauvoo a mud hole. Even so, she wasn't prepared for what she saw. The weather had been wet all week, and the so-called streets of Nauvoo were bogs in places and practically rivers in others. She saw quite a few houses, but they were mostly cabins scattered about; and in between the houses the dense growth of trees and underbrush made the place appear a virtual jungle. The sky was overcast, but the heat was miserable — and it was only June. How could she survive this place?

People in town looked happy enough, not the sad, crazy sorts Justin had talked about. But they looked poor. Their clothes were worn and muddy.

The wagon, which had been rolling and pitching about in the mud, finally came to a complete stop. The horses stood shaking and breathing, unwilling to push ahead for the moment. "We'll all have to get down," Matthew said. "I may have to unload to get through this mess."

"Oh, Matthew," Mother said. "Not in all this filth."

"I'm sorry."

Ruth didn't hesitate, didn't complain. She hiked up her skirts and stepped down onto the mud and felt her boots sink into the mire above the ankle. But she didn't even look down. She slogged through the muck onto slightly higher, drier ground, and then reached out her hand to Mother, who was following. Matthew got down on the other side of the wagon and began

121

shouting at the horses and slapping their haunches with the ends of the reins.

The horses drove hard and slipped about, but they stumbled forward and pulled on through the deepest, worst of the mud. "We'll have to walk from here," Matthew said. "There are some other bad spots up ahead."

By the time Matthew stopped the wagon in front of the place he assumed must be their house, Ruth was muddy up to the top of her boots, and her skirt was a mess, too. She was too busy watching her step to notice that Joseph had come out to greet them.

"Mother," he said, "hello. I'm sorry you arrived when the mud is so bad. Really, it's not been like this in a long time."

"It'll dry up," Mother said, but she sounded less than happy.

"Yes. And turn into ruts so deep nothing will pass over them. But that's one of the things that will have to be taken care of this summer. Brother Joseph says we can't do everything at once."

Ruth was standing behind the wagon and still breathing hard from the difficult walk. She was ankle deep in mud. Joseph had been glancing at her, but now he finally motioned for her to come to him. "Come over here where the mud isn't so bad. Take a look at the house I've built for you."

Ruth had looked but hadn't given much thought to what she had seen. When she looked more closely she realized what Joseph meant when he said "for you." It was a two-story house, and it had a front porch. It was a log building, but he had tried, as well as he could, to build a house like the Hemsteads'.

"You've done quite a job here," Matthew said, and he did sound pleased.

"I got a lot of help. People came in last winter and used up all the logs I had cut. I think they felt obliged to make things right. Most folks couldn't see why I wanted such a big place, an upstairs and all, with only the four of us, but I told them I would have things right for my mother and little sister."

He looked at Ruth again. "There's a room upstairs, like the one you and Mother had on the farm, with a window so you

can look out on the city and the river. But it's a room just for
you. You'll have a bed all to yourself." And then he smiled.
"Only I couldn't do anything about the bed yet. I had no money
for furniture."

"Joseph, I have good news about that," Matthew said. "Mr.
Hemstead felt he owed us something for the work we've done.
He gave us this wagon and team, and he had us bring along
some pieces of furniture. Besides that, he gave us three hundred
dollars. We can make things right with Brother Joseph about
this land, and then we can fix things up in the house. Whatever
is left I want you to have. You've worked up here a whole year,
and you've ended up with nothing to show for it."

"No, no. I can't take any of that. That's the family's money."

"You deserve your share of it, Joseph," Mother said.

"Sure. My share, the same as all of us. It goes into this land,
and maybe a piece of land outside town to start a farm."

Matthew stepped a little closer to Joseph and put his hand
on his shoulder. "Joseph, Mother and I have talked about it.
We know you have no feel for farming. We think you should
learn something else. A little money might give you a start at
something."

"Matthew, I don't feel right about that. I lost what I earned.
If I hadn't done that, I would have some money now. It's not
fair for me to do something that stupid and then come to you
to replace it."

"Joseph, that's not how I see it. You worked for Mr. Hemstead, same as I did. And you came up here and nearly lost
your life trying to get something started for us. That one mistake
doesn't mean a thing compared to all that."

Ruth was watching Joseph and could see his confusion, but
she also saw his appreciation. Approval from Matthew had always meant a great deal to Joseph, no matter how much he
struggled against him at times.

"Well," Joseph said, "we'll have to talk about all that. But
come into the house. I want you to see it. I've not quite finished
all the floors, but I've done enough to show you how it will be.
No dirt floors for us. With some of that money you brought

along, we could put up clapboards and paint the whole place white. And we could plaster inside. You would hardly know it was a log house." He was looking at Ruth again, smiling, and she knew he wanted her to smile back. She did try.

They all had to take their boots off to go inside. Ruth could see that Joseph really had done a fine job. He had arranged the rooms somewhat the way the Hemsteads' house was, although the place was not nearly so large. Surely, it was the nicest place the family had lived in—except for the Hemsteads'.

Joseph slipped away for a time early that evening. He didn't say where he was going. He had still not even mentioned that the Engberts were in town, let alone that so much had passed between Mary Ann and him. He just couldn't tell Matthew yet, and especially not Mother. They would think he was too young, that he had too much to do before he could provide for a wife. Of course, he knew that himself, but it didn't change the way he felt about Mary Ann.

He asked Mary Ann to walk out with him a little. "In all this mud?" she said, winking.

"Well, we can take a little air out front."

"If the air doesn't kill us." All the same, she did walk outside.

They had no more than made it out the door before Joseph said, "Mary Ann, my family got in today. Mr. Hemstead gave us three hundred dollars. Mother and Matthew want me to have part of it."

He saw her eyes widen and the smile that meant she was pleased.

"I don't feel that I can accept too much of it. They need to get started here. But even fifty dollars might be enough to put money down on a lot."

"We could raise enough on the lot to get by until we could get money ahead to buy a farm."

"That's what I had been thinking too. But Matthew said something to me today that got me thinking another way. Matthew said my heart's not really in farming, and that's true. It never has been. I was just trying to think of a way for us to get started."

"But what could you do?"

"I'm not exactly sure. But I know I like to build. Some of the folks who gather here will want to hire someone to build a place for them. I could maybe do that. Or there might be other businesses I could start up. I learned a lot about keeping books while I was in New Orleans. And I learned something about the way a good business works."

"But Joseph, it takes money to start a store, or a mill, or—"

"I know that. But I've been thinking all afternoon. Maybe I can start by just hiring out—glazing windows, putting down puncheon floors, plastering walls. And then I could—"

"Joseph, you never plastered a wall in your life." She laughed and shook her head.

"Well, sure. But it can't be all that hard to learn. If there's someone around here who's done it, I'm sure I could watch a little and get the idea."

"But could you make a living at it?"

"Well, I could do lots of things, enough to make a living from it all. There's carpenter work—building cabinets, making furniture. With some practice, I think I can do any of those. And then maybe I'll set me up a business in one of those trades. In time, I think we'll see plenty of brick homes here. It might be that a brick mason might do just fine. And if I had five or six masons working for me, I could keep books, bid jobs, take care of the business itself."

"And sit at a desk in a fine suit and walk about town, tipping your stovepipe hat to all the pretty young ladies you see."

"Well, yes. That would be nice." But when he saw her double up her fist and shake it, he added quickly. "No, no. You know I'm joking. This is for us, not just for me. I don't think it would take that long for me to get started. I could advertise in the *Times and Seasons* right away that I can build log houses and put down floors. Then the first chance I get, I'll start learning some of the other things I need to know."

"What will Matthew think about all this? Won't he need help?"

"No. He'll get some land, and he'll farm. That's what he loves."

"And what's so bad about farming that you don't want to do it?"

"I don't know, Mary Ann." He looked past her now, down toward the river. "I've just always wanted to do something that didn't tie me down to one thing, so much the same all the time. I've been down the river and back—twice now. Matthew never has gone, never even wanted to."

"Maybe it was worth the trip, Joseph. You did learn some things."

"I learned not to get dunked in the water by the same folks you're trying to baptize." But that's not what he was thinking. He was thinking there had been reasons to go after all. He'd come to love the Book of Mormon; he'd worked at something other than farming, and been successful. And despite everything, he felt more sure of himself than ever before. He had trusted his feelings, and he hadn't been wrong.

Ruth was standing in her room upstairs—by the window, where she had liked to stand at the Hemsteads' place. She could see the big arch in the river, and she could see the last of the sun's rays. She could also see the silhouettes of trees along the riverbank. In this light, Nauvoo seemed quite a pretty place. But the air was stifling and humid, and the mud was still out there, hidden in the dark. She thought about the Hemsteads, and about Justin. She was quite sure she would never see him again, no matter what he had said. She wished now that she had been a little more kind to him there at the last.

More than that, she wished she were older. She would soon be thirteen, but Mother still treated her like a little girl. The whole family did. If she were sixteen, or maybe eighteen, she could do so much more to choose her own way. But eighteen was a long way off—too far even to dream about. Dreams were silly anyway. They were fine for Emmie; she liked dreams better than real life. But Ruth wanted things she could hold fast. Too many things in her life had slipped away from her already.

Maybe Nauvoo was not so bad. The mud would dry. The house was quite nice. "But they won't let us keep it," Ruth said to herself. "They'll come again. They'll take this away, too. Then where will we go?"

Chapter 19

The Williams family had only been in town a few days when Joseph Smith stopped by one evening. He stood in their house and looked around. "You've done a fine job here, Joseph," he said. "This is more what we should be building now—nice, large houses with lots of windows for light. We're not a little band of people holing up in shanties and cabins anymore. A house like this says to the world, 'We plan to stay right here.' "

He walked on through the house, talking with Mother about her ordeal in getting out of Missouri and about the house where she had lived since then. "Well, I know that wasn't easy to give up," he said. "But here you're with your people. I think you'll find great joy in that."

"I know we will, Brother Joseph."

The Prophet stopped and looked around at the family. He had thrust his hands down in his pockets. As usual, he was wearing no suit coat. "You folks have paid plenty. I hope you'll find peace here." Ruth thought he was looking at her. He stepped toward her and put his arm around her shoulders. "I'm sorry you've had to suffer so much in your life."

Ruth had not been prepared for this, and she felt something give way as she heard the kindness in his voice. It was as though Father were back, the father she hardly remembered, but someone strong and good who could make everything safe.

Brother Joseph spoke softly, sounding unusually solemn. "We've got our problems here in Nauvoo." He looked at

128

Mother, and then at Matthew. "I know you can see some of them, and others you'll know about in time – but don't let yourself become too disappointed. We'll make this the best place on earth. We'll have a fine time, too. We're going to have social halls and theaters and a university. We'll have enough dances and parties to keep even a beautiful young woman happy."

He looked down at Ruth. "There'll come a time when you'll feel sorry for any girl who has to live on a miserable old farm down in Quincy."

Ruth was amazed. How did he know? Had Joseph said something?

"Brother Joseph," Matthew said, "there's something I want to tell you. Ruth wasn't any too happy about coming up here – as you seem to know – but I didn't want to come, either. I wanted to keep the farm. I agreed to come because it's what Mother wanted, and that's about the only reason. But now that I'm here, it does feel right. I like seeing so many good people hard at work. I like what's happening to the city. I'll do my part to build it."

"That's good, Matthew." Ruth could see that Brother Joseph was very pleased, even moved, by Matthew's words. "You'll be a great help here. All of you will. There would have been nothing wrong with your staying where you were. But I do think you'll feel a part of something important now. Nauvoo may not look like much yet, but if the people can just get the right vision, it can be a blessed place."

Ruth felt the Prophet's hand begin to turn her toward him. He looked into her eyes. "I know what you're feeling these days. But the time will come when you'll be thankful you came. I can promise you that." He gave her shoulder a last squeeze, and he nodded firmly, and then he walked to the door. "One other thing. You're going to hear some bad things about me here in Nauvoo. I have enemies. I hope that those of you who have known me the longest will think the best of me. I hope you'll trust me."

"Don't worry about that," Mother said. "We're not about to turn on you now."

He nodded and said, "Thank you, Sister Williams. But I'm afraid I'm not as good a man as I would like to be. I've disappointed too many people."

"From what I hear," Joseph said, "too many have disappointed you."

Brother Joseph looked down for a moment. "I guess you mean John Bennett. But I still think he can be a friend. He's done a good deal for us." He thought again. "Our biggest problems are still right here. Governor Boggs, over in Missouri, won't stop chasing me just because we beat him once. But he doesn't worry me nearly so much as some of the people in Nauvoo who can't accept me for what I am. We've got people around who believe the first bad thing they happen to hear about me or the Church and then spread every rumor, no matter where they hear it."

The Prophet was hinting at something. Joseph had heard some rumors, but nothing he believed. He wondered why Brother Joseph seemed so concerned. "Did anyone ever figure out who it was who shot at me?"

"I'm afraid we had too many candidates. We have managed to chase a few of those out of town."

"It was just a few days after that when I got sick. I don't think that dive in the river did me any good."

"No, I'm sure it didn't. But I don't think the illness hurt you any—not in the long run. You've grown up an awful lot in the last year, Joseph. I've seen the change."

Joseph knew what the Prophet meant—knew what the time in New Orleans had done. But he was very pleased that Brother Joseph had noticed it.

"Joseph, could I speak to you privately for just a moment. Could you step outside with me?"

Joseph was taken by surprise, but he walked outside with the Prophet. "Joseph," he said, "in the last few days I've had some thoughts about you. I came here tonight to make a decision—and the Spirit has told me I was right about you." He stood for a moment, looking into young Joseph's eyes. "It's time for you to serve a mission. I feel a spirit about you that tells me you're ready. And the Lord needs your service."

Joseph took a step back. He felt as though he had been shoved.

"Don't look so shocked. You've always known this was coming. This is just the first of many missions for you."

Joseph could think of nothing to say, but Mary Ann was mixed up in all his jumbled thoughts.

"I would like you to go back to the country you came from — New York and on up into the Northeast. I want you to preach and baptize, the same as any missionary, but I also want you to stop in every branch and ask the members to hasten their gathering. We have men up in that country who own farms and homes, but they don't want to give them up. They want to stay where they are. They need to sell those farms and turn the money over to the Church. We can provide new lots for them and some land to farm, but we need the money right away. We have notes coming due and not a way in the world to pay them. You've just given up a place of your own — or one that could have been yours. I think you'll carry the right spirit with you."

Joseph was hardly hearing, hardly thinking about the Prophet's words. He was only thinking about leaving again.

"Will you do it?"

Joseph had no answer ready. He knew he had to say yes, and yet it was not the answer that was in his head.

"What's the matter, son, are you frightened?"

"Some, I guess."

"Well, don't worry about that. You're twenty now, aren't you?"

"Nineteen."

"That's fine. That's old enough. Some of those farmers would look me in the eye and say, 'I ain't moving one foot from this spot of land,' but a young man like you comes to them, and the same man says, 'I feel right about this. It's what I have to do.' "

The Prophet waited again, but still Joseph couldn't think what to say. The cicadas were buzzing, and insects were whirring about in the night. For Joseph, it was as though all the buzzing and whirring were in his head.

"You'll go, won't you, Joseph?"

"I'm not sure it's the right time, Brother Joseph."

"I thought about that. But Matthew can get your place established and take care of your mother and sister. I think maybe it's one of the best times in your life to get free. When you get a little older, you'll have more obligations, and getting away only gets harder, I'm afraid."

"I guess I have something of an obligation now, Brother Joseph."

"What's that?"

Joseph took a breath. "No one knows this. Not even my family. But I've asked Mary Ann Engbert to marry me."

The Prophet laughed softly and nodded, seeming to understand. "No wonder you look so white in the face. It's love that's making you weak-kneed."

Joseph laughed, embarrassed, but he was a little bothered that the Prophet took the matter so lightly.

"Well, now, love can wait just a little when it has to. A year wouldn't do any harm to either one of you. You're both young. You could get married first, if that's what you have a mind to do, but I suspect it would be better if you just kept your engagement for that time. You weren't going to get married right away, were you?"

"No, I wasn't. I don't know when we can manage it. But I need to get something established—get some money ahead for land or to start up a trade."

"Joseph, all those things work out all right. But they don't matter very much compared to building up the kingdom of God. I think you know that."

"Yes, I do."

"Then you'll go, won't you?"

"I'm not sure."

The Prophet's head snapped back a little with surprise.

"The problem is, Brother Joseph, Mary Ann's father thinks she's silly to wait around for me. There's an older brother in town—Brother William Hall. He already has a place and a trade. Brother Engbert thinks Mary Ann ought to marry him." Suddenly Joseph smiled. "Couldn't you call him instead of me, and give me a chance to do some catching up?"

Joseph Smith smiled. "The Lord told me to call you, Joseph, and I'm not about to tell him that he's made a mistake. Stop by my house tomorrow and tell me what you've decided. I'll give you that long to think about it." He slapped at a mosquito that had landed on his neck. "I *have* been tempted to ask the Lord why he created mosquitoes and sent so many to live here in Nauvoo—but I guess he has his reasons for that, too." He laughed, and then he walked away.

Joseph stood in the door for quite some time. He didn't want to go back in and tell his family what had happened. If he did, he would have to explain his hesitancy. He still didn't want to do that.

Suddenly he was walking, heading for Mary Ann's house. When he got there, he knocked on the door and then asked her to come outside. "Joseph," she said, with that playful smile of hers, "if I keep standing about with you at night, the neighbors will start to talk."

"Don't tease with me tonight, Mary Ann. I have something serious to talk to you about."

She stepped outside and shut the door. "What's the matter?" she said. "You look upset."

"I am—a little. The Prophet just came to see me. He wants me to leave—soon—and go on a mission. He wants me to go for maybe a year."

"That's good," Mary Ann said. "It's an honor to be called on a mission so young."

But Joseph saw that the blood had drained from her face, and he heard the strain in her voice. "I know, Mary Ann. It is an honor, but I didn't tell him I would go. He told me to think about it for a day."

"Joseph, you have to go."

"Maybe not. Maybe I could ask for a delay for a time and promise to go in a year or two. Right now I feel I've got to look after some other things. A man has to live, too. He can't just run off on missions all the time."

"Joseph, you *will* be going on missions all the time. I've always known that."

Joseph had known it, too. But he had never put that reality together with the one he was trying to create with Mary Ann. They had talked about his business hopes, the trade he might develop. How could he ever get anything started if he spent his life always preaching? He looked at those soft eyes, the ones that weren't teasing now, and he wondered how he could spend his life leaving them. He had told Ruth she would live on cornbread and prayer someday; suddenly he saw himself providing the same kind of life for Mary Ann.

"I don't want to go right now. I have so many things I want to get started. I was hoping by this time next year we could get married. If I leave now, in a year I'll only just be starting again. And someone else might be opening the very kind of business I want to start."

"Joseph, you wouldn't turn the Lord down, and you know it. There's no use even talking about it."

"Mary Ann, I'm afraid you'll get married while I'm gone. Your father would still rather see you marry Brother Hall. I'm afraid if I leave he'll talk you into it. Or you'll meet someone else you like better than either one of us."

"Joseph, you know me better than that. Or at least you ought to. I've promised you. I'll keep my promise." Tears were in her eyes.

Joseph didn't want to cry. He was entirely too old to cry. And yet the tears were coming. "I love you, Mary Ann," he said.

She nodded, and the tears rolled down her cheeks, silver in the moonlight. In a moment she mumbled something Joseph couldn't understand.

"What?"

"It's one of those times."

"One of what times?"

"When you really ought to kiss me."

"No, it isn't. I'll miss you all the more if I let myself do that."

And so they just looked at each other. "I'll find a way," Joseph said. "Maybe we can still get married soon after I get back. I'll try to figure out something."

"I'll wait, Joseph. I won't ever settle for anyone else. I'm so proud that you're the one the Prophet chose."

Joseph walked back home, and he told his family everything. He told about the missionary call, and about Mary Ann, and about his promise to her.

Matthew took Joseph in his arms and told him he was very proud. "You'll be a good missionary," he said.

Mother hugged him too, and she cried. "I've known this time was coming, and I'm happy for you, but I do hate to have you leave us again so soon. I've missed you so much all this last year."

Then Ruth hugged him. She clung to him and cried. She said not a word, but sobbed and sobbed. Mother watched, and seemed concerned, maybe even confused, but Joseph thought he knew at least some of what Ruth was feeling.

Chapter 20

"Brother Joseph, I'm willing to go." The Prophet looked up from his desk and smiled. "I guess you knew that all along," Joseph added.

"Never had a doubt." He stood up and shook Joseph's hand. "Take a day or two—whatever you need—to get things in order, and then come back to see me. I'll ordain you an elder."

"Brother Joseph, Matthew is not an elder yet. Would it be right to—"

"His time is coming. There's no need to worry about that."

"All right. I can be ready to go in a couple of days. I'd like to get going as soon as I can."

"So you can get back sooner?"

Joseph smiled and looked at the floor. "Well, I suppose that is part of what I'm thinking. Could you say more exactly how long I should stay?"

The Prophet looked at him for a moment. "I'll leave that up to you. The Spirit will guide you. Do what I've told you to do, and then come back. But stay no longer than a year."

"I'm not sure I know exactly what to do."

"We'll talk more about that. I may find you a companion to send along, too. I have some people in mind."

"All right. I'll come back day after tomorrow."

"Good. Don't spend your time fasting and praying. Once you're on your way, you'll get enough fasting without meaning to. And you'll pray plenty—more than you ever thought of praying before."

136

"I've prayed quite a bit this last year."

"Yes. I guess you have. It shows in you too, Joseph. You're a man now. I always told you that you had work to do in fulfilling God's plan. This is only the beginning."

Joseph shook the Prophet's hand again, and he turned to leave.

"Oh, one last thing," Brother Joseph said. "When you get back, I'll make a plot of land available to you. You'll pay for it whenever you can. But I don't want you to keep that poor girl waiting too long. I think you should marry her soon after you get back."

Joseph went straight to Mary Ann and told her what Brother Joseph had said—and he told her right in front of Sister Engbert. She smiled, congratulated them, and then she left the room. Joseph took the chance to fold Mary Ann in his arms. She nestled so comfortably there that he didn't hold on long. "I'll see you this evening," he said, and he hurried home.

Matthew was not there; Mother said he was out buying lumber to build some of the furniture they needed. Joseph told his mother that he would be leaving in a couple of days, and then he broke down and told her everything—what Joseph Smith had said about Mary Ann, and about the building lot.

"Joseph, I'm happy for you," Mother said, but she looked concerned.

"Is something wrong?"

"I'm worried about Ruth. She's upstairs. Why don't you go up and talk to her."

Upstairs Joseph found Ruth looking out her window. He could see that she had been crying. "Are you all right?" he said.

She nodded, but that was all. Actually she had been wanting to talk to Joseph, and yet she wasn't sure what it was she wanted to say.

The room was still empty for the most part, except for the few things the Hemsteads had given Ruth. She did have a small trunk, and Joseph had her sit down on that. Then he sat on the floor and leaned against the wall. "I'll be leaving in just a short time, Ruth. Maybe the day after tomorrow. I've been telling you that we need to talk. I think maybe now is the time." Joseph thought she was finally ready. He saw something in the quiet way she was waiting. But she still said nothing.

"Ruth, last winter I prayed for Mother and Matthew every day. But especially I prayed for you. I kept asking that you would begin to see what this city means. I guess that hasn't happened yet. I saw the way you looked when you were standing out there in the mud."

"Joseph, I can't help it if I don't feel the way you do — even if it's the way I'm supposed to feel."

"Just tell me what you do feel."

"Scared."

"Scared? Why?"

"I don't know."

"I thought it was the mud and the log houses. I thought you wanted to have pretty dresses and go to fancy parties. That's what you told me before."

"I do want those things."

"And you're scared you'll never have them?"

Ruth had never addressed the question quite so directly. She was not sure what it was she was always seeking. "Joseph, when I was a little girl, I remember those men who came, and they screamed and yelled and called us names. I don't remember when they hurt Father. I don't remember much of the rest, but I remember them yelling at us. And then I remember being cold, always cold. I remember getting so wet in the rain, and being in a tent, and being so cold I thought I would never get warm again."

"Do you remember Father at all?"

"Yes. A little. I remember sitting by a fire, and he was holding me in his arms. He had big, black whiskers and a deep voice. He held me close, and I had my head against those whiskers. And then he wasn't there anymore. In Far West, when the men came back and yelled and threatened us — I remember all that — I used to wish we still had him. I would pray at night that God would send him back. Instead, we ended up in our wagon, and it was always so cold, and no one could even stop little Samuel from dying. I always thought Father could have kept him warm."

Joseph had known all this, and yet he had not realized how much of it was still in Ruth. He had been frightened, too, but he had been older.

"I want to be safe, Joseph. I don't want anyone to hurt us anymore."

"We're safe here, Ruth."

"I don't think so, Joseph. Even the people who like us best — Emmie and Mr. Hemstead — think we're sort of crazy. They don't think we should all come to one place and make a city for Mormons."

"I know. They don't understand what we're trying to do. But that doesn't mean they'll try to hurt us."

"Maybe *they* won't. But some will, I'm afraid. Mr. Hemstead said that people are turning against us again — just the way they did in Missouri."

"We have an army here, Ruth. It's going to be a big one. There will be thousands and thousands of us. No one will try to run us off again. Besides, most people like us here in Illinois."

"I don't think so. Not really."

"Ruth, part of my mission is to go out and bring more people here. Every time another family moves in we are a little stronger. That's why we had to leave the Hemsteads'. It's not just the strength to drive off our enemies; it's also the strength of the Spirit. You heard Brother Joseph say so."

"I want to live in Boston."

"Why Boston, Ruth? What's so nice about Boston?"

"I've read about it in the newspapers. The people live in nice houses made of brick, and they dress nice and speak nice."

"And no one burns down houses and drives people out into the cold."

Ruth nodded. That was it, as childish as it sounded.

"Ruth, there are bad people everywhere. But just think of a whole city of people looking out for each other, trying to live God's plan, putting the gospel first. There's nothing more safe than that. We all just have to want it enough. Every single person has to want it and strive for it."

"Joseph, I don't feel that way. It never seems to happen. Too many people can't do it. And too many people hate us for trying. I just want to be like other people."

"Oh, Ruth, that's the way I felt at your age. I would have given anything not to be different—not to be a Mormon."

"What made you change?"

"I knew I had to be in or out. I couldn't try to walk a line down the middle."

Ruth shut her eyes. She felt a relief come over her. She had to say it. "I think I want out, Joseph."

Joseph took a deep breath. "I don't blame you for feeling that way, Ruth. But will you do something?"

"What?"

"Will you try really being 'in' before you give 'out' a try?"

"How do I do that?"

"Did you pray this last year the way I asked you to?"

"Some. But I don't think I wanted answers, Joseph. I don't like to be bossed."

Joseph smiled. "Even by the Lord?"

She didn't reply. She couldn't even look at Joseph.

"You're so much like me, Ruth. Everyone told me to pray when I was your age, but I didn't want to. I knew what I wanted and I didn't need to ask about it."

At least he understood. But Ruth suspected that she was more wicked than Joseph, more rebellious.

"Will you try to be a part of Nauvoo, Ruth? Will you pray about it, and will you try?"

"I don't know, Joseph. I don't know how."

"Look for chances, Ruth, and don't fight the good feelings you get. Alma told the people they would never find joy in their costly apparel." Joseph smiled. "He told them to try just a little faith and see whether it didn't feel right. He said it was like a seed that could grow. Can't you try that? Can you just try to believe and see whether it doesn't feel right to you?"

"Yes." And though she spoke quietly, she knew it was something she wanted to do. She sat on the trunk and looked at her hands. Joseph could see tears starting again. "Joseph, I don't want you to go. I miss you when you're gone."

"Ruth, I don't want to go. It's the hardest thing I've ever had to do."

"I thought you wanted to be a missionary."

"I do. But not right now."

"Because of Mary Ann?"

"Yes."

"Do you love her, Joseph?" She smiled a little, but the tears were still coming.

"Yes." Joseph couldn't look at her. "That probably sounds silly to you. When you're twelve, love seems kind of stupid."

He didn't know. Ruth wouldn't tell him that part. It was the thing no one would understand — not Mother, not Matthew, not even Joseph. She could tell them she had given up plenty already to come to Nauvoo, but they would think the idea funny. She was not even thirteen.

In a few minutes Joseph left. Ruth sat in her room alone. She thought about the Hemsteads, and Emmie, and Miss Gordon and the school, and Justin. And then she did what she liked to do when she felt sad. She got out her beautiful blue dress, held it before the window, and let the light shimmer off it. She missed Mr. Hemstead terribly. She sat down with the dress and held it close to her, felt the smooth coolness of it. "I'll never wear it now," she said.

But this was not helping. She put the dress back in the box and put the box away. Later, when she went to bed, she tried to think about the things Joseph had said. She got back up, knelt down, and prayed.

Ruth was gone much of the afternoon the next day, and when she came back her mother was concerned. "Ruth, you said you wouldn't be long. It's been almost three hours. I was starting to wonder what had happened to you."

Mother sounded angry, more than concerned, and this was not easy for Ruth to take. Not now.

"Where have you been, Ruth?"

"I had something I wanted to do, but it took me longer than I expected."

"Do? What did you have to do?"

Ruth was surprised how hard it was to say it. "I sold my dress."

"Your dress? You mean the blue one?"

"Yes."

"Sold it? Why?"

"I'm grown out of it." But the words brought tears.

"Ruth, I don't understand."

"I want to give the money to Joseph. For his mission."

"Oh, Ruth. You didn't have to do that." And now Mother was crying. She took Ruth in her arms. "I lost my beautiful china—back in Jackson County. But at least I have a few of the broken plates."

Ruth understood what Mother was trying to say. "I love you, Mother," she whispered.

"Oh, Ruth. It's a fine thing you've done."

"I have to try," Ruth had been telling herself all day, but that didn't make it easy. She had hoped she would feel good about selling the dress, happy she was doing something for someone else. It was her way of entering the city. But as the man had taken the dress and handed her the money, she had almost backed out. She had felt no joy at all.

"It's the right thing, dear," Mother was saying.

Ruth thought maybe it was, but the emptiness was still there. She went upstairs and looked out the window, out across Nauvoo and the river. She saw rutted roads that were supposed to be streets, and she saw shacks and cabins where the city was supposed to be. She cried because she would never wear the dress.

It was then that she heard someone step into the room. She turned and saw Joseph, who was standing with his arms outstretched and with tears streaming down his face. She went to him, put her arms around him, and clung to him for a long time. "Oh, Ruth, thank you," he kept saying. "It's the finest thing you could have done."

Ruth wasn't happy—not yet. But when she stepped back from Joseph, something had changed. She felt sure that she had done the right thing.

Joseph seemed to know. "It's the seed," he said. "It will grow now. I promise you."